COSEGA
STORM

COSEGA
STORM

Brandt Legg

LAUGHING RAIN

Cosega Storm (Book Two of the Cosega Sequence)

Published in the United States of America by Laughing Rain

Cataloging-in-Publication data for this book is available from the Library of Congress.
ISBN-13: 978-1-935070-08-5
ISBN-10: 1-935070-08-8

Cover designed by: Jarowe

PUBLISHER'S NOTE
This book is a work of fiction. Names, characters, places and incidents are products of the author's imagination or are used fictitiously. Any resemblance to actual persons, living or dead, businesses, events or locales is entirely coincidental.

BrandtLegg.com

For Teakki and Ro

one

Tuesday July 18th

Soldiers had surrounded the house. Ripley Gaines and
Gale Asher had known Grinley for only a day, when he'd
shoved them into a dark, dusty passage under the house in
the high desert of New Mexico. They'd followed it to its
end at a sheer cliff six hundred feet above the Rio Grande
River. Automatic gunshots echoed off the canyon.

Gale felt as if the narrow tunnel walls were closing in
on them. A week ago she'd trashed her life, as a successful
writer for National Geographic; by following Ripley
Gaines, the world-renowned archaeologist, on a daring
flight to protect an ancient artifact. The things he'd
discovered in the mountains of Virginia were so
controversial and valuable that FBI and Vatican agents
were relentlessly hunting them. More than a dozen people
had died since the find and she was, at least partially, to
blame.

"We're trapped," Rip growled.

"Maybe the soldiers won't find the tunnel. We can just
hide down here until they go away."

"They know we were in the house. They'll tear it
apart. They'll find the tunnel entrance. They'll be here any

minute. We're finished." After a week of running, Rip had finally snapped.

Gale sat down on the rocky floor. Her wrist throbbed from a fall minutes earlier. She wiped the blood trickling down her arm and leg. "We could go back up and maybe . . . Rip, bring the flashlight, quick!"

Rip scrambled down from the tiny opening. "What?"

"I think the tunnel turns."

Rip scanned the wall next to her and saw another shaft. It couldn't have been more than eighteen inches wide and five feet high, but it was a passageway.

"Come on," Rip said, helping her up. Squeezing into the new tunnel required removing their packs and considerable twisting. The darkness swallowed the flashlight's beam as the walls continued to narrow ahead. They held their packs, stooped, and pushed into the black.

Nanski and Leary, the two Vatican agents tracking Gale and Rip, had taken shifts for the past twenty-four hours; one slept at the hotel while the other watched the San Francisco de Asís Mission Church, both unaware of the FBI agents watching them.

"This is the day. We're going to finally catch Gaines and Asher." Nanski said as they met up. "I've been praying on it."

Leary pushed a second stick of spearmint gum into his mouth. "Why are you so sure they'll come at all, let alone today?"

"As I've told you before, if they're in Taos, they came here for one reason, to find Clastier."

"I still don't understand how they expect to find a long-dead, humiliated priest?" Leary absently traced his fingers around the cross- etched in the hair at his temple.

"You haven't studied the mysticism of Catholicism or you'd know that the answers we seek are always surrounding us. They want to know about Clastier; he was here and so his answers are here."

"Yeah, well, we're here too, so I don't think they'll get the chance to find answers at the church. But I'll happily arrange a personal meeting for Gaines and the late Mr. Clastier. Hope they don't have any trouble finding him in the crowds of hell."

two

The FBI had tracked Nanski's credit card and obtained his plate numbers from a hotel in Albuquerque. Now agents were following both Nanski and Leary, hoping they would lead them to Gale and Rip. Because of interference and corruption from the Attorney General's office, and the NSA's interest in the case, the FBI Director had tapped into DIRT, a long-classified section of the Bureau. The acronym stood for "Director's Internal Recon Team." The select agents were handpicked by the Director and operated outside the Bureau's normal protocol and procedures. Two of DIRT's top operatives had been assigned to tail Nanski and Leary.

The senior agents in charge of the investigation, Dixon Barbeau and Wayne Hall, ate breakfast burritos a few miles from the church in a private conference room at the New Mexico State Police district headquarters. They were in direct contact with the DIRT surveillance team situated around the church.

"Clearly, the Vatican agents didn't capture them in West Memphis," Hall said. "It's damn frustrating that not only do we need to apprehend Gaines, but with our own Attorney General working against us? Then we also have to waste time working around a couple of religious roughnecks who are trying to beat us to the artifacts." He poured more coffee. "I want to arrest those Vatican boys in the worst way. I know why we have to wait, but eventually, when we're sure we can keep them behind bars; I'm going to enjoy bringing them in, even more than getting Gaines."

Barbeau studied the map of New Mexico on the wall. "Why Taos?" he asked, mostly to himself. "Why would two of the most wanted people in the world bring three stolen artifacts to Taos, New Mexico?"

"Where else should they go? Taos has a large anti-establishment community. Maybe they've got friends here who can hide them." Hall, just trying to keep the conversation going, knew the Bureau hadn't turned up any connections in Taos to either Gaines or Asher.

"Why not flee the country? Booker Lipton is one of the richest people in the world. We know he's involved in this mess. Why hasn't he whisked them off to some part of the world outside our reach?"

"There may be places beyond the reach of the Bureau, but is there anywhere in the world where the Vatican doesn't have influence? Does a place exist where the NSA can't get to someone?" Hall asked, rhetorically. He'd felt from the beginning they were missing something. One of the top archaeologists in the world stealing an artifact is strange enough, but the week-old case had spun out of control. Agents from the Vatican were killing witnesses; and interference from the White House, NSA, and the Attorney General's office made it difficult to keep track of all the moving pieces.

"Maybe we should pick up Booker Lipton?" Barbeau asked.

"Think we can find him?"

"He's a smart man, I'm sure he's well out of the country, but the Director is working on it through higher channels."

Hall nodded as he skimmed the manuscript of Gaines' upcoming book, *The Future of the Past*. After the murder charge went public, his publisher quickly complied with the subpoena, and the PDF had hit Hall's inbox the night before.

"It's well written, accessible. Makes archaeology seem exciting, like all the answers to the world's problems can be found in the past," Hall said. "I'm only eighty pages into it, but I have to say it again: Gaines could make more money lecturing and writing, kind of the Stephen Hawking of archaeology. So why throw it all away?"

"And I'll tell you *again*. He got greedy and he didn't think he'd get caught."

"Where did that first lead come from? I mean, I was on my way to the dig site hours before he'd committed any crime. How did we know?" Hall asked.

Barbeau dropped his fork and swallowed a bite of green chilies hard. "Jesus, I never gave it a thought. There's nothing in the file," he said, dialing the Director's number. "How could we have known so fast?" Barbeau repeated while waiting for the Director to pick up.

Hall continued to read Gaines' manuscript while only half-listening to Barbeau's side of the conversation with the Director. He noticed a new email – the Bureau had received a second document containing edits that had been removed from the final version of *The Future of the Past*. A note explained that the sections on Gaines' controversial Cosega Theory were being saved for his next book due out a year later. Hall opened the PDF and began reading.

"According to nearly all my contemporaries, prior to the existence of what is generally accepted as the first human society, approximately 50,000 years ago, there is no fossilized record of intelligent man. That absence of proof, as so often happens in science, has become proof. Without evidence to the contrary, the majority of anthropologists and archaeologists have accepted the narrow hypothesis that humans were not evolved enough to establish a society prior to that point in time. I disagree and find it interesting that in religion, the absence of proof is called faith, and yet in science the absence of proof simply creates proof for something entirely different – whatever fits the most popular theory."

Gaines' writings went on to detail the current version of the history of man. *"Our earliest recognizable ancestors showed up four to six million years ago. Until roughly 200,000 years ago, during the Middle Paleolithic period, anatomically modern humans evolved from Homo sapiens. And it wasn't until about 50,000 years ago that the emergence of language, culture, and basic technology happened. Truly modern humans, using agriculture, have been around only 10,000 years or so. But what if that's all wrong? What if in all those millions of years another society existed?"*

Hall looked up and considered the question, then returned to Gaines' argument. *"There is considerable evidence to support a radically different thesis. Tools found in England dating back more than two million years; others in Argentina that are three to five million years old; modern human footprints in volcanic ash dating to three point six million years ago. Bones of anatomically correct humans found in multiple locations from two to four million years in the past. Many more tools are over hundreds of thousands of years old in Africa, Lake Huron, and Mexico. Finds disputing the current views number close to a thousand. Too much evidence to ignore."*

Hall found the list surprising. Gaines was bucking the entire scientific community. There were pages of footnotes backing his claims, but Hall knew the most important proof was probably what Gaines had pulled from the cliff in Virginia. "What did he find?" he whispered to himself.

Gaines' narrative grew bolder. *"As the evidence mounts, I believe we are on the brink of discovering an artifact that comes from the gap periods, something that cannot be swept away. And it is my contention that this impending discovery will not only show intelligent human activity, prior to the accepted timelines, but rather it will show an advanced civilization, which vanished. The question is no longer, what if it's wrong; the question is, how wrong is it?"*

Hall glanced at the photo of San Francisco de Asís Church on his laptop screen. It was no wonder the Vatican didn't like Gaines; they were barely comfortable with evolution, and this crazy archaeologist wants to prove the existence of something akin to the New Age dream of Atlantis. But the bigger question at the moment was, if what Gaines found proved his Cosega Theory; then why not just come forward? The Vatican and Gaines were both acting as if much more were at stake than the founding dates of some ancient settlement.

Barbeau hung up the phone and looked at his orange juice, as if appalled there wasn't vodka in it. "The Director believes the initial tip came from a Vatican source working at the dig site."

"The Vatican coincidentally had an agent on an obscure dig in Virginia?" Hall asked.

"It wasn't an obscure dig. It was a Gaines-affiliated excavation. And it wasn't an agent. The Director says there is evidence that the Vatican covertly places young church loyalists on digs around the world. Because of his notoriety and controversial theories, the digs of Ripley Gaines are likely the highest priority."

"Highest priority for what?"

"Don't you get it? The Vatican expected something to be found. And they thought it likely Gaines would be the one to find it."

Hall looked back at the image of San Francisco de Asís. "What the hell did he find?"

three

Kruse, a security specialist for Booker Lipton, stared at the tattoo of three bullets penetrating a heart that covered his right wrist – and waited for his boss to answer the phone.

"Are you in Taos?" Booker asked.

"Yes, sir. Is Gaines?"

"We're almost certain he is. And so are the FBI, NSA, and Vatican agents. You've got to find him first."

"Why is he here?"

"He must be trying to figure out the artifacts. There is a Taos connection."

"Any idea why he hasn't called you?" Kruse asked with the detachment of an intelligence operative trying to collect all the facts necessary to do his job.

"He's scared they'll find him."

"That's why he should call." Kruse operated from logic. It was his only religion. Trying to understand the emotions and impulses of people wasn't easy, but if he had enough facts, knew enough about them, it was possible. "Why is he trying to figure out the artifacts when he should be hiding in a country without an extradition treaty?"

"I think he knows his life is over. Hiding may only prolong it a very short time. No one wants to prosecute him; everyone wants him dead. The artifacts are the only things that can save him."

"The town of Taos has about 6,000 residents and fewer than a dozen stop lights. The NSA, FBI, and Vatican employ the highest technology and intelligence methods in existence. Their agents are the best trained in the world . . . Gaines should last about ten minutes in this town," Kruse said.

"You've got to be better. Harmer is on the way to help. Her plane lands in twenty minutes. Be there to meet her. My pilot will remain on standby; he won't leave the airport in case you need a speedy exit. Let's hope you do."

Kruse shook Harmer's hand. They'd worked together once before; he remembered the cough. She remembered his tattoo – the three bullets representing the three people he'd killed, but the heart was his. Although denying the deaths haunted him, he did admit each did a little damage to his heart. The tattoo had originally featured only one bullet, after his first kill, but had been designed to accommodate many more.

"Never figured why a bright woman like you smokes," Kruse said.

"They're addictive," Harmer said, defensively.

"Ever hear of mind over matter?"

"Yeah, if it doesn't matter, mind if I smoke?"

"Keep the window down."

Booker called as they were leaving the tiny airport. "Bad news. There's a standoff. NSA has Special Ops surrounding a remote, private residence not far from you.

Gale and Rip are believed to be holed up there. Shots have been fired from inside the house. Here's the address."

Kruse wasn't sure exactly what they were supposed to do and hoped they'd be able to get a good view. But from his experience, if Gale and Rip really were in the house with Special Ops present, they would likely be dead or in custody, even before Kruse and Harmer arrived.

The NSA commander on the scene had strict orders. Attract no attention and preserve the artifacts. Using lethal force was expected but tricky, given the directives. If the targets were still in direct possession of the artifacts, killing them would be the safest way to insure the items' protection. Tough mission. In addition to retrieving the artifacts, his orders were explicit – keep them from falling into the hands of FBI or the Vatican agents.

With each minute that ticked by without surrender, the potential for failure rose, raising attention, other agencies arriving, the media; a brewing stew of uncertainty. The commander had men stationed to cover all exit points, property parameters, as well as hiding in two strategic trees. He resisted calling in air support because of the attention it might cause and the unpredictability it added – the artifacts were the mission. The instant shots began coming from the roof, things got way more complicated. The commander stood looking at what he called a "funky fortress" and wondered what kind of freak would live in such a bizarre building. He knew the man's name, Willard Grinley, and he knew his arrest record, but understood nothing about him.

"Sir, we've confirmed the man on the roof is Grinley," a soldier told the commander. "We may have a shot; should we take it?"

"Why would this nut bag take in two notorious fugitives?" the commander asked, ignoring the question.

"They probably don't get much news out here, sir. Maybe he didn't know. Maybe he did it for the money."

"Then why fire on us? He could have just claimed he didn't know who they were."

"He'd have no way of knowing who we are. Maybe he thinks we're from a Mexican drug cartel. He's tangled with them in the past."

"Take the shot, but only if it's Grinley. Gaines and Asher need to be taken alive until I know where the damned artifacts are."

"Yes, sir." The soldier already knew Gaines and Asher were not to be killed, but the commander didn't like mistakes. He relayed the kill order.

Grinley didn't know who the soldiers were, but knew they were after his new friends and not him. And clearly they weren't there to make an arrest. These soldiers came to kill people. "Get off the roof now," he said to himself. He'd been able to set all the gun turrets. Now he could shoot from the safety of the house. Thick adobe walls protected him, at least until the invaders decided to use heavy artillery. He sat in his control room and counted seven soldiers on the small monitors, but knew there were more that his cameras were missing.

four

Gale and Rip continued along the side tunnel for another hundred yards. The walls were so close together that Gale wasn't sure they'd be able to turn around if it led to a dead end. The heavy air felt thick enough to see, but she couldn't see anything. Rip's body blocked the weak flashlight beam and she bumped into his back when he stopped unexpectedly.

"That might be daylight ahead." Rip sounded desperate. He clicked off the flashlight.

"I hope so," she said. They tried to move faster, every so often stepping on something slimy. Finally, an opening in a narrow shaft appeared above them, impossible to reach.

"Can you boost me up?" Rip asked. There was no way for her to get in front for him to raise her up.

"I'll try." She managed to get him high enough so he could grab hold of a crag, while his foot balanced on a narrow ledge

"It's like a chimney. The opening is too small," his voice strained. "Wait, the rocks are loose." He pushed some of the smaller ones away. "I think the entrance was intentionally covered up."

"Can you see out?" she asked, still worried they might be in the gorge.

"Not really. Let me move some more." Rip wedged his body against the wall behind him and used his right leg to push away the larger stones. Some of the smaller pieces hit Gale so she moved back into the tunnel. A few bigger chunks landed inside. "I'm through!" he yelled. "We're in some kind of ravine, the gorge is about fifteen feet away."

"Thank God," Gale said. She handed their packs up to Rip; then was able to climb partially up on the stones that had fallen through. He reached to pull her up. They laid there gulping the sagebrush-scented air and relishing in the sunshine.

"We have to keep moving; they could be right behind us," Rip said.

Gale looked back into the hole they'd just come from. "I doubt it."

"When they find the entrance . . . " Distant gunshots interrupted him. The contours of the mesa made it impossible to see Grinley's house, but it was still too close. Rip yanked the gun, flashlight, and envelope from his pockets; and stuffed the gun and light into his pack; and opened the envelope. "There has to be thousands of dollars in here."

"What?" Gale said, leaning over to look. "Why would he give us all this cash?"

"I dunno. Guess he knows what it's like being a fugitive." More shots came from the direction of the house. "Come on!" Rip headed north along the edge of the gorge. Another burst of gunshots had him breaking into a jog.

"If they're still shooting, that means the soldiers haven't found the tunnel yet," Gale said.

"*Yet* being the key word."

Half an hour later they spotted a dirt road descending a series of switchbacks into the gorge. "I see a bunch of cars down there by a bridge. Maybe we can hitch a ride?" Rip said, breathlessly.

"Did you forget you're wanted for murder?" Gale asked.

"And I'm armed," he said, motioning to his pack where he'd stowed Grinley's gun.

"We've got gas money. We'll figure something out."

By the time they reached the bottom, it had been close to ninety minutes since Grinley had pushed them into the tunnel. Gunshots punctuated a dire fate for the old man who had so eagerly helped them. Gale looked back for a second, clenched her fists and pushed on.

The cars all seemed to belong to people on balloon rides, or latecomers to a rafting trip. A school bus with a trailer full of river rafts was unloading by the water. Rip considered trying to steal a car, but even if he could get one hotwired, driving a stolen vehicle was likely the dumbest thing a wanted man could do.

"Why don't we get on a raft?" Gale suggested.

At first Rip dismissed the idea but then thought it could be the perfect escape, depending on how far they went and assuming he wasn't recognized. They wandered over to a young guy with a clipboard. Just before they reached him, Rip whispered to Gale, "Maybe you should do the talking."

"Hi," Gale said. "Any chance we're not too late to join the fun?"

The guy looked the sweaty and dusty pair over and narrowed his eyes. "Is that blood on your shirt?"

"I fell climbing some rocks," she pointed to the cuts on her arm and gashed leg. "It looks worse than it is."

He nodded. "These trips require reservations."

"We didn't expect to be in town today." She found his eyes and smiled.

Rip marveled at how she worked.

"It's a seventeen-mile epic over endless flies of Class III and IV rapids. It's been a super wet year; we'll even hit a few Class V."

"Do you have room?"

"We did have a group of four cancel this morning, too late to pull anyone on the waiting list."

"Great!" Gail squealed.

"Yeah. Well it's $150 a person."

"Did you keep the payment from the other group?"

"Yeah, but . . . "

"How about $200 for both of us?" Gale asked.

He looked over at Rip who was trying to look as innocent as he could. "Either of you been down Class V before?"

"The Rogue, the Cheat, Snake, Colorado," Gale said.

The guy looked impressed and turned back to Rip.

"I did the Noce River in Dimaro a few years back," Rip answered truthfully.

He nodded. "Okay. Cash?"

Rip pulled out two hundred dollar bills, silently hoping they weren't counterfeit.

"Do you have a few wet-bags? We've got some papers with us that need to stay dry. Like I said, we didn't expect to be hitting the river today."

"Sure; she can get you bandaged up, too." He pointed them to the bus where a pretty college-aged girl was excited to use her first-aid skills; she cleaned and wrapped

Gale's leg, then took care of her arm. They gave fake names on the release forms and tried to remember them. They got enough Ziplocks, plastic, and duct tape to protect the Clastier Papers, his laptop, and especially the Eysen – the eleven million year-old, hi-tech artifact that had everyone hunting them.

Rip unzipped the legs off his convertible pants; Gale was already in shorts. They both wore their packs over the life jackets against the protests of the river guide. After a quick orientation and introductions, each passenger was handed a helmet and an oar, and they were underway.

Rip couldn't help but look skyward for an expected helicopter. As they eased through the calm waters below the John Dunn Bridge, Gale and Rip tried to relax. There were four rafts, six people in each; they rode in the last one.

five

A state police captain explained to Barbeau and Hall that shots being fired on the mesa were nothing unusual. "Someone likely doing target practice, maybe shooting a coyote or what not. But you wanted to be told of every report."

"Do you have officers responding?"

"Yes, sir, but it'll take him twenty-five minutes to get there."

"Can we get a unit in the air?"

"That'll take more than an hour, with your clout, maybe a little less."

"We're in a Third World Country," Barbeau said to Hall.

"He's having a bad day," Hall said to the captain.

"So, you're saying he's not always so rude and arrogant?" the captain asked irritably.

Barbeau laughed. "No, Captain, I'm always rude and arrogant. My apologies to you and the great state of New Mexico."

The captain nodded and left the room.

"What's your gut say?" Barbeau asked Hall.

"Why would Gaines draw fire? He's unarmed."

"Maybe the Vatican has more agents and they're killing Gaines right now. Or worse, maybe the NSA has found him."

"If he came to Taos for some kind of research, would he be out in some remote house? Unless maybe Booker has a property here."

"Taos is the Wild West, the final frontier . . . you can bet Booker has a place close by."

"Call the Director."

"Right," Barbeau said. "Meanwhile, peel one of our guys off the church stakeout and sweet-talk that state police captain into giving you the address where the shots were fired."

The Director told Barbeau that DIRT had been working on Booker from day-one and so far all they had learned was that Booker had a talent for hiding and keeping secrets. They did, however, come up with some new and startling news; Gaines wasn't the only one with important friends. Gale Asher and Senator Monroe were very close. Barbeau hung up more puzzled than ever.

"Senator Monroe, the presidential candidate?" Hall asked.

"Is there another?" Barbeau barked. He pulled a folded map from his pocket and carefully placed it on the table. Virginia and Washington, D.C. were printed on one side. He already had red dots marking: Gale's house, Rip's Harper's Ferry place, Josh Stadler's house, Ian Sweedler's lab, and the location of his body, the dig site, and now he added a dot to the U.S. Capitol building. It comforted him to see it all in front of him. Another map charted their course along the parkway to Asheville through West Memphis and on to Taos. They both had the same information on their laptops, but Barbeau liked the feel of map paper, enjoyed making marks in ink, and highlighting roads.

"But Senator Monroe is a big-time Catholic, maybe not quite up to Attorney General Dover's standards, but still he makes Kennedy look like an atheist," Hall said.

"I know this." Barbeau moved a long clear ruler around the maps.

"Well, the obvious conflict . . . DIRT tells us that the senator and Gale Asher were once lovers and are still close friends. Don't you find the coincidence disturbing?"

"Sometimes coincidences are just that."

"I don't like them. Coincidences are always a sign of trouble. Look at the facts. Have you ever seen or heard of the Vatican being this aggressive on anything? Ever?"

"No."

"And the presidential front runner, a devout Catholic with deep ties to the Church, is a former lover of one of the two people at the center of the turmoil."

"Nothing about this case is normal - Booker Lipton, the Attorney General, the NSA – I wouldn't be surprised if the British Royal Family files an expired colonial claim on their former Virginia colony, and sends troops to recover these damned artifacts."

Hall almost smiled. "Be that as it may, we need to question the senator."

Grinley had seen trouble from Colombia to Chicago, and accumulated vast tactical experience from plenty of street scuffles and guerilla-type fighting. His prison time, and many years spent moving drugs across the Mexican border, contributed to his knowledge and fearlessness. Every time he saw a soldier twitch, he fired a single shot toward them. Grinley was careful not to kill any of them, fearing that it would result in an immediate siege. He wanted a standoff, not a massacre; it was all about buying time.

For more than an hour, the commander was convinced that Grinley, Gaines, and Asher were all shooting at them. Shots came from all six turrets, but no shooters were spotted. The imaging and heat scanning equipment were producing inconsistent results. Their visuals had too many blind spots and the frustration level increased with each shot. Normally, he'd wait until nightfall, but once word came through that the state police and the FBI were minutes away, he ordered his men to take the roof.

six

The river guide had the rafters practice paddling through the riffles during the first few miles of the trip. "It's a seventeen mile run, and after yesterday's monsoon, this could be extra fun. If it gets rough, pay close attention to my commands. Big Class V excitement! Let's be careful."

Gale made friends with a couple from Des Moines who agreed to give them a ride into town after the trip. Soon, the water began churning and they navigated rapids called "Ski Jump" and "Dead Car." Gale kept searching the sky for choppers as the raft pulled and jerked through the white water.

When they entered the Power Line rapids, she realized this was no simple river. The guide told them that they were lucky the water was at its highest level in years. "Lucky?" Gale asked sarcastically. Twice she slipped as water pelted her and the raft bounced off rocks. White water swirled up and around as the rafts were pummeled through the winding canyon. Rip even briefly forgot their pursuers as he fought to stay in the raft.

They were relieved to reach a calm section and stop for lunch on the banks of the Rio Grande. Self-conscious that everyone would think they were fugitives, Gale made animated conversation about past river trips; while Rip nervously scanned every direction. The deep gorge provided only a narrow view of the sky six hundred feet above; still he worried that agents would scale down the cliffs at any moment.

Another group of rafts appeared up river. Rip, certain they were filled with FBI agents, moved closer to the shore, and his only hope of escape. Gale found him.

"It's just another party of rafters," she said.

"How do you know?"

"Because no one knows we're on the river."

"Yeah, like they didn't know we were at Grinley's."

The rafts floated to the edge and guides pulled them onto the beach. Rip studied the occupants tensely before agreeing that they were harmless tourists.

Back into the water, they were alerted to upcoming serious Class V conditions, and the Rio Grande came to life again. "Rock Garden!" the guide called, and Rip vaguely remembered some sort of warning they'd been given about this stretch. Suddenly, they were sideways and went over a submerged boulder. The raft came down, almost folding in front. Rip knew the angle was dangerous as the raft tipped high out of the water.

"We're going in!" someone yelled.

Rip grabbed at the upper side. Water slapped at him. At the last second, an eddy caught the waterside of the raft and spun them back level. The excited cheers of his raft mates signaled it was over. Rip exhaled and looked to Gale. Clearly shaken, she was checking her pack. He did the same, just before they went pounding through another set of rapids.

They hit the Rio Bravo rapids where the river descends seventy feet per mile. The Rio Grande was raging. Rip was concentrating so hard on trying to stay in the raft that for the first time in more than a week, he forgot about the Eysen. Even the guide looked tense as they tore through the wild waters. It felt as if the river were trying to swallow them, like a furious serpent chomping at fat little bugs.

Rip stole a glance ahead and saw a seething foaming swirl that no sane person should attempt. But what lay just beyond that took his breath. A recent slide had narrowed the river into a horrific funnel that the raft could barely squeeze through. It was obviously a new obstacle; as the guide was already looking for a way out of the river; there was none.

The swirl pushed them in two harrowing three-sixties before spitting them into the funnel. It sucked them in with such a violent force that Gale, Rip, and another man slammed into the river guide at the back of the raft. Like a bullet, they shot out of the funnel. The force propelled Gale over the side. As she disappeared into the fierce froth, Rip lunged forward and tried unsuccessfully to spot her. In the same instant, with a skilled and practiced move, the guide leaned backwards over the edge of the raft, extended his arms an impossible distance, and pulled Gale back into the raft.

While the guide continued to navigate them through the treacherous waters, Rip steadied Gale as she gulped in air. "Are you okay?" he yelled over the thunder of the river.

"No. I think so."

"You're shaking."

Before she could answer, the raft caught air and spilled them both backward. They barely managed to stay inside low slick walls. The guide kicked Rip and pointed toward more rapids. "Worry about her later, I need you paddling."

Breathless, Gale and Rip got back in position and helped keep the raft pointed forward and level; leaning and paddling whenever the guide ordered. Soon the river eased to Class IV and III, eventually it flowed to a calm Class II.

Once at the take-out near the Taos Junction Bridge, they staggered to shore, soaked and exhausted, but relieved by their escape.

seven

Booker's security force known as "AX," was becoming increasingly involved in the situation. No one knew was sure AX stood for, but the smart and loyal army of agents would do *whatever* Booker needed done.

Kruse and Harmer, were the two lead AX agents assigned to find Gaines and Asher. The odd couple had watched the raid on Grinley's from a safe distance. They were out of their league with the elite Special Ops unit, but at least they would be able to report to Booker what had happened. Their view wasn't great, as scrubby juniper and cedar trees were concentrated around the house. However, two gun turrets were visible from their vantage point, parked behind some large chamisa bushes, half a mile away. The state police and the FBI had passed their dusty pull-off with hardly a glance.

At first they were surprised, when they heard shots fired from the house. It seemed out of character for Gale and Rip to be fighting back with automatic weapons. But Harmer had pointed out that the fugitives were trapped, and it was their final stand.

"I wonder how Gaines and Asher wound up at this whacked desert outpost?" Kruse had asked.

"Probably a decent hideout. If it hadn't been the NSA after them, they might be eating chips and salsa now, instead of being part of a shoot-out," Harmer said, lighting a cigarette.

As the hours wore on, and no arrests were made, they were baffled. "Maybe the spooks got bad information. Is it possible Gaines was never in there?" Kruse asked. "I mean, we've been watching the whole area. Nothing has moved on the mesa."

"Then who was shooting back?" Harmer asked.

"Some poor Second-Amendment-militia-separatist-freak, who probably thinks the government has finally come for his guns." They both laughed. "I better call Booker."

"I haven't heard anything from my source," Booker said. "You're telling me that they haven't gotten them?"

"Soldiers are in the house and no one has come out."

"Maybe they're dead?"

"Possibly, but no shots were fired once the soldiers entered."

"They could have escaped?"

"We've been scanning the whole area since we got here; there is not a perfect view of the house, but we can see the surrounding sagebrush in all directions."

"I'll make some more calls and get back to you. Let me know if anything changes," Booker said.

"Roger that."

"God damn it, Rip," Booker said to himself after he hung up. "Call in!"

It took a couple of hours before Booker finally got word that the raid had been a bust. The tunnel gave renewed hope that Kruse and Harmer might still get to Rip first.

"How lucky can one guy be?" Kruse asked, hearing the news.

"Apparently pretty lucky, when he's walking through desolation toward destiny."

"What does that mean?" Kruse asked.

"It means find him. Tell me what else you need. We're running out of time."

Thirty minutes later, Kruse and Harmer were parked at a central location, waiting word. Gale and Rip were, miraculously, still on the loose. Booker was betting they hadn't left Taos. Kruse believed remaining in such a small town would be an idiotic move, but one that fit with the professor's previous steps. They spent the next few hours watching   traffic.

"I may not be impressed with how he's done it, but I sure as hell am amazed that he's done it," Kruse said the following morning as he and Harmer drove up and down Paseo del Pueblo.

She looked over at Kruse and understood why Booker sometimes called him the Commando. He looked so military – cropped hair, lean, and muscled build. She never could tell the color of his dark eyes, which were usually hidden behind shades anyway. Harmer glanced at the number "3" scratched into the barrel of his Glock-19, lying on his lap. He was always playing with his guns. The poor guy is a mess, she thought. She liked messed up people and might have made a play for him, if men had been her preference.

They turned onto La Posta Road and took it to Ranchitos, not really expecting to find anything, but wanting to be ready. They'd spent the night in a chain hotel and were well rested.

"I still can't believe they escaped through a drug smuggler's tunnel, " Harmer said. "I would love to have seen the look on the Special Ops guys when they found an empty house."

"The bigger question is where did they go?"

"Hopefully, the boss has some new intel for us. As yesterday showed, it's going to be damn near impossible to beat the feds on this."

Kruse called Booker. "Did you get my wish list?" he asked.

"We're taking care of it. We should have it completed by tomorrow," Booker said.

"If there is a tomorrow. Any new leads?"

"As far as I know, our three competitors are eating breakfast, and waiting for something to stir," Booker said. Kruse knew that by "three competitors" Booker meant the FBI, the NSA, and the Vatican.

"I'm surprised we're not all bumping into each other. If he's still dumb enough to be in Taos, I'll bet you a hundred bucks he doesn't survive the day, without one of us getting him."

"Make sure it's us," Booker said, ending the call. He leaned back in his chair and stared at a wall of computer monitors, frustrated that his vast wealth and various connections had, thus far, failed to get him what he most wanted.

eight

The river trip had taken more than three hours, and by the time the Des Moines couple dropped them at the Taos Plaza, almost six hours had passed since Grinley had pushed them down the tunnel. They were sure the soldiers had killed him.

They ducked into a sunglass shop, paid cash for shades and ball caps, and anxious to get off the street, stopped at the motel on the plaza. Rip was impatient to check the Eysen for damage. Gale hoped the TV might have news of the raid and Grinley. The clerk told them there were no rooms available. They hurried toward another motel several blocks north. Everyone looked suspicious.

On the way, Gale ducked into a vegetarian restaurant for takeout. Rip waited outside and leafed through the Taos News, a weekly that came out on Thursdays; already outdated, it had nothing about him. He found a USA Today at another paper box and scanned it as they walked. There, on the bottom of the front page, accompanied by his standard six-year-old publicity shot, was the headline, "Famous Archaeologist Sought." The story quoted an Assistant U.S. Attorney who said that Gaines was wanted for the murder of Ian Sweedler, a lab technician. It had become a federal case, the story said, because the alleged murder had been committed in connection with possible theft of undisclosed government property.

"The bastards are framing me. All the government has to do is accuse you of murder, and you might as well be guilty. No one is going to believe I'm innocent," he said.

"But you weren't there. I'll testify that you were with me."

Rip stopped walking and looked at her. "Gale, you'll be dead."

She stared back at him. He regretted saying it. Her eyes, like his, were hidden behind dark glasses, but he saw the pain in her expression. No more words were spoken until they reached the motel.

It was set off the main road, Paseo del Pueblo Norte. Gale checked in using Grinley's cash and another new name. As soon as they locked the door of their ground-level room, Rip checked the Eysen and his laptop. Remarkably, everything seemed fine; although there wasn't enough sunlight remaining in the room to make the Eysen come to life.

"The papers are safe and dry," Gale announced. "Hey, maybe you shouldn't turn on your laptop?"

Rip pulled his finger back from the power button. "They can't trace my computer, unless I check my email or login somewhere."

"Are you sure?"

Rip looked over his computer and saw no trace of moisture. "I guess there's no need to chance it." He turned on the TV instead.

They ate dinner watching the cable news coverage of Gaines. The segment was filled with footage from his many appearances on news programs. One commentator said, "I know Professor Gaines, and I must say these allegations are shocking." Several colleagues being interviewed agreed, saying that the charges were impossible. The story didn't mention Gale – only that Gaines was traveling with an unidentified woman.

"See, some people believe you're innocent," Gale said.

"Maybe a few old friends."

Exhausted, Rip fell asleep, while Gale showered. She made some notes in her journal, but didn't last much longer. They woke just after four a.m., when Rip cried out from a heart-pounding nightmare. Gale reached across the king-sized bed they shared and found his hand in the darkness.

"We're safe," she said, quietly.

It took him a minute to remember where he was. "How do they keep finding us? No one knew we were at Grinley's."

"Tuke and Fischer did."

"So first Booker turns us in, and then an ex-con and a truck driver betray us?"

"All I know is if we don't know who to trust, then we shouldn't trust anyone."

"We need friends, Gale. We can't get out of this alone."

"We're not alone," she squeezed his hand. He hadn't noticed she was still holding it.

"I can't do a war zone romance," he said.

"Romance? I thought we were talking about needing *friends*." She pulled her hand away.

"Sorry, I . . . "

"Don't worry about it." Gale laughed. "If you weren't so average-looking and unintelligent, I might consider it," she added, sarcastically.

He forced a laugh and sat up. "Coming to Taos was a mistake."

"They would have found us anywhere."

"I'm calling Booker."

"No, wait. Please, give me today. We're here. Clastier is waiting. He brought you here across the centuries. Let's see what he wants."

"He wanted me to find the Eysen. And I've done that." Rip got up and moved the curtains to look outside. Only a few dim lights disturbed the early morning darkness; nothing stirred.

"You know it's more than that. We saw Clastier in the Eysen yesterday!" she said.

"Yesterday, we killed another man. Grinley is dead. We haven't even admitted that yet. I'm tired of causing this trail of death."

"You're not to blame. We're just trying to get away," Gale said.

"I know, I know. And if we stop, we'll be killed too."

"We've seen the Eysen. They won't let us live."

Neither spoke for a moment. Gale walked into the bathroom to brush her teeth, grateful she still had some basics in her pack.

"Okay," Rip said. "But we're not sleeping in the same place twice. We leave Taos tonight."

nine

The commander had been stunned to find an empty house. It had taken just over an hour to find and disarm booby traps to gain entry; then twenty minutes to find the tunnel, forty-five more to disarm additional bombs, and another twenty minutes to follow the tunnel. There was no trace of *any* of them.

The New Mexico State Police arrived before they had penetrated the dwelling. Even then, he had a bad feeling. When the police officer asked for credentials, the commander reacted badly and had his men take the trooper into custody. Before the same *faux pas* could be repeated with the FBI; the commander contacted Washington, and the agent withdrew.

It was nearly dark when they finally left the house. If Grinley ever dared to return, he would find it empty. Most of the contents had been trucked away as evidence. The arrested trooper was released. It took intervention from the governor to avert a public relations nightmare.

The commander briefed his superiors of the embarrassing failure and the information was conveyed to Busman, the NSA's man in charge, who was still in the nearby town of Angel Fire. He took the news well, these things happened, which is why he always had a Plan B. Should that plan fail, another was waiting to be tried.

Sean Stadler had been escorted off a Greyhound bus, in Asheville by the NSA. Because he was the younger brother of the now-dead photographer, who had taken the pictures of the artifacts at the dig site, and because he'd helped Gaines and Asher get out of Virginia, the fugitives trusted him, and the NSA needed him. He knew things.

It had been Busman's idea to pull Sean in, and he considered the mission important enough to do it himself. Although Busman was only five-foot, seven inches tall, he seemed a little taller, maybe because he was a fitness fanatic, and as he said, "I'm in beyond-perfect physical condition." A precise man, he also said he had two point three children, but the point three were actually three Doberman pinschers.

Busman had moved Sean and his handlers to Taos. Sean had been going crazy; confined to a cabin in the woods. The thirty-minute drive through Taos Canyon and his hotel room in town were a welcome change of scenery. They even complied with his request for doughnuts, and bacon, for breakfast; the same breakfast shared with his girlfriend, after their first overnight. He missed her and promised himself that whenever this was all over, he would propose. No one knew that Sean's hotel was less than a mile from Gale and Rip's.

Priorities changed after the botched Grinley raid. The NSA picked up a conversation between high-level Vatican officials discussing Gaines and one of the artifacts. The Church's description of what they called the *Ater Dies* was stunning. "With the new information from Rome," Busman's superior told him, "Gaines' surviving the raid was a good thing. But it means we've got a bigger problem;

other than just getting to Gaines before the FBI or the Vatican."

An NSA computer, scouring millions of phone calls in the areas where Gaines had traveled since finding the artifacts, had turned up a call between him and fellow archaeologist Larsen, in which the artifacts were mentioned. That, coupled with other data the intelligence agency had uncovered, indicated that what the Vatican called the *Ater Dies* was one and the same as what Gaines had named the "Eysen."

"So we need Gaines's knowledge to acquire a complete understanding of the purpose, meaning, and workings of the Eysen?" Busman asked his superior.

"He's crucial."

"That might be a little tricky, with the FBI and the Vatican also pursuing," Busman said.

"Tell me what you need. This is SAB."

Busman didn't need to be reminded; he felt the pressure of the *Scorch And Burn* assignment every waking minute and knew nothing was out of bounds – breaking laws, assassination, – whatever it took to achieve the objective, to get the Eysen, and now bringing Gaines in alive, with it. Plan B would need to be modified and Sean Stadler might have to be sacrificed. He jumped rope for twenty minutes; it helped him think.

Barbeau wasn't surprised to hear of the NSA's fiasco on the mesa. He'd already started calling Gaines "Houdini" and this was at least salve for his bruised ego. If the mighty NSA couldn't capture the professor, when they had him completely surrounded by a Special Ops unit, then the Bureau's misses didn't look so bad. And, more importantly, Barbeau needed to be the one to bring them in, or something terrible was going to happen. He hadn't figured out just what that was, but he knew enough to know the situation was becoming more complicated every hour.

This case felt desperate; he wasn't just in a chess match with Gaines, but was also waging a battle with anxiety. Over the past fifteen years, it hadn't been just the Bureau changing; the entire government had become so obsessed with stopping terrorism, that long-established checks and balances had been eroded. But this one was even worse; it was as if the rulebook had been burned.

ten

Wednesday July 19th

After a forty-minute walk, Gale and Rip reached the Taos Pueblo a few minutes before it opened at eight a.m. The cool summer morning air, a reminder of the high desert, carried a hint of wood smoke.

"I've read about it and seen photos, but it's more than I imagined," Rip said as they stood on the banks of the teeming Rio Pueblo, a wide and shallow creek that had provided drinking water for centuries.

"It's as if it was sculpted out of the earth." Gale marveled at the turquoise doors and layered adobes stacked on top of each other five stories high.

Rip imagined what it would be like to excavate such a site a thousand years from now. The earthen walls would leave little trace; it would be the plastic, metal, and ceramics that might give a clue. But what if that didn't exist? What if it had been properly disposed of and nothing had been left behind? What if he was excavating such a site; ten thousand years from now, a hundred thousand, or a million? Nothing would remain.

The tour guide, a young native woman, gave a brief history as she led them toward a beautiful five-story adobe structure at the base of Taos Mountain. The light earth-colored buildings against the pine-covered mountains, wrapped in the bluest sky, were a breathtaking sight. "I can see why this place inspired Clastier to write," Gale whispered to Rip, as the tour guide began her talk.

"Our ancestors lived in this valley long before Columbus stumbled on America and hundreds of years before Europe emerged from the Dark Ages." The tour guide swept her arm out before her. "It is believed that the main part of these buildings were constructed between 1000 and 1450 A.D. When the first Spanish explorers arrived in 1540, Hlauuma, the north house, and Hlaukwima, the south house, would have appeared much as they still do. The Spaniards believed that our pueblo was one of the fabled golden cities of Cibola. It's the oldest continuously inhabited community in North America, and a UN World Heritage Site."

Gale and Rip, the only ones on the tour, nodded appreciatively. In their line of work, they were both familiar with the Taos Pueblo.

Rip had grown up reading Clastier's writings, the bulk of them done at Taos Pueblo from where Clastier made his final escape attempt. Gale had been consumed by his papers for days, and was obsessed about discovering the connection to the Eysen. On the walk to the Pueblo, they reviewed all they knew of Clastier, and considered what might have happened to him once he left Taos. The Church had a posse after him, but there is no record of his capture. In fact, beyond the papers in her pack and those left behind in Asheville, no proof of his life existed at all.

"Any questions?"

"What religion is practiced at the Pueblo?" Gale asked, wanting to get into the church.

"The majority of my people are Catholic. We practice that, along with the ancient Indian religious rites."

"Don't the two conflict?" Rip asked. Gale nudged him.

"No. The Pueblo religion is very complex. The two are interwoven like the white and brown threads in my blouse – together they make a beautiful fabric."

Rip figured she'd heard the question before and decided not to bring up the fact that Catholicism had been forced on her people; things hadn't been going so well since the Church had woven itself into the fabric of their culture.

"Could we see the church?" Gale asked.

"Of course. On the way, we'll just stop at some of the shops, so you can see the insides of the houses."

"Do people still live here?" Gale asked, trying to sound touristy.

"Oh, yes. About one hundred and fifty people live full-time within the old Pueblo village. Another nineteen hundred Taos Indians live on our surrounding lands. You'll like the shops. We're famous for our mica-flecked pottery, moccasins, and drums. There are many wonderful artisans here."

Rip was impatient to get into church across the way. A crudely painted board next to the shop's entrance read "Wood Crafts."

"Remember," the tour guide began, "within the Pueblo walls, tradition dictates no electricity or running water are allowed."

She was right, Rip thought, as he stumbled into the shop, the only light coming from the small narrow doorway. Rip had to take off his sunglasses to avoid walking into anything. A dozen carved masks, flutes and walking sticks were on display; another rack held a few pipes and a small glass case of trinkets. He was about to leave when; the proprietor, a very wrinkled Native American man, smiled at him. Rip smiled back. Then the man's toothless expression turned angry. He stabbed his bony finger into Rip's chest.

"How dare you return here?" The man grabbed a stick and shook it at him. Rip immediately assumed the man recognized his picture from the news, and was ready to flee, when Gale stepped between them.

"What's wrong?" she asked, looking directly at the old shopkeeper.

"You cannot stop him!" the man yelled at Rip, ignoring Gale.

Their tour entered. "Grandfather, Grandfather. It's okay." She patted his shoulder then turned to Gale. "I'm sorry. He sometimes thinks he sees things that are not there."

"No. It is true," the man shouted. "I was Tagu, I was there." He glared at Rip.

Gale and Rip froze and shared a desperate glance. Clastier's closest friend at the Pueblo had been named Tagu.

eleven

Grinley had spent the night in a friend's yurt. When the soldiers hit the roof, he was already in the tunnel. There were enough remote controlled and timed weapons to keep them busy for a while. They'd find it much easier to blast the back door, than to try bulletproof windows, or the reinforced steel plates on the roof. And he was right. By the time they gained access, nearly an hour had elapsed. Grinley had already made it to the main road with a duffle of cash and two cell phones. A friend picked him up and dropped him at an old pool hall, where he waited for someone else, who drove him to a back road, where a third buddy waited – the one who owned the yurt. Grinley, an old paranoid drug dealer, was determined never to return to prison, nor to be killed by his enemies. He had so many escape plans; he couldn't remember them all.

At the New Mexico State Police district headquarters, Barbeau and Hall sipped coffee and waited for another break, as the sleepy little town came awake. At least, it appeared that the Vatican agents had been right – Gaines was in Taos. But it troubled him when Hall pointed out that no one had actually seen Gaines since he'd left the dig site.

Word of the raid on Grinley's compound reached Nanski and Leary long after it ended, because of a new system Barbeau and the Director had implemented. Tired of the Attorney General keeping the Vatican updated on the case, Barbeau and Hall now reported developments to a DIRT agent first, and waited as long as possible before entering the normal chain of command, which would lead quickly to Dover. Trying to keep the NSA out of the loop was, as the Director put it, "a whole other monster; the NSA, by design, is beyond the reach of anyone."

Leary sucked on a successive series of wintergreen Lifesavers, while Nanski worked the phone – first the Cardinal in Rome, and then Pisano, his Vatican contact in the states. Leary was more bored than tired. Nanski was neither, but his nerves were wearing thin. Perhaps more than anyone, he knew the stakes. No one, especially the NSA, could be allowed possession of these artifacts, or the Church would be destroyed. Each passing day brought the greater risk of more people learning the astonishing secrets. Nanski knew a point existed when killing people would no longer protect the Church, and he feared that point was very close. Too many agents were in Taos trying to get the artifacts.

Leary watched in awe, as Nanski strategized and continually tried to anticipate Gaines' next move. But Nanski was frustrated; either little evidence of Clastier's life remained, or Rome was purposefully keeping it from him. The high-ranking Cardinal, who had been feeding them information, was also navigating a mysterious world of competing interests and egos. "Power is not something you hold; it's a fluid and dangerous thing that can turn on you at any time. This is particularly true in the complex world of the Holy See," the Cardinal had told them.

Senator Monroe needed to be the next call. Pisano had talked to him, but Pisano didn't grasp the magnitude of the situation. Nanski punched the Senator's private number into his cell.

"Senator, I hope you don't mind if I get right to the point. I know about your relationship with Gale Asher, and was hoping you could tell me something about her that might help us anticipate their next move."

The Senator had been expecting the call, but Nanski hadn't been expecting his response. "Listen to me, Nanski. You've bungled this thing from the start. I've always believed the Vatican had one of the best intelligence outfits, but I'll bet a couple of amateur private eyes from the yellow pages could have caught them by now. There is only so much I can do to help your cause, but I can tell you this: there should be no question as to where Gale's loyalties lie."

twelve

"My grandfather sometimes lives between two worlds," the Pueblo tour guide said.

Gale looked back over her shoulder at the centuries-old buildings. "Can we just talk to your grandfather?" she pleaded.

"I don't think that's a good idea," the tour guide said, as they approached the church. She had had to practically push them out of his shop while holding her grandfather at bay. "I've never seen him so upset."

"He called himself Tagu," Rip said. "Who did he mean?"

"That's not his name. I've never even heard it before. Please don't think too much about what he says."

"Does he see past lives?" Gale asked.

The tour guide stopped and considered Gale for a moment, before walking into the church's courtyard. "Let's not discuss these things any more."

Gale was about to speak, but Rip raised his hand just enough to catch her attention and waved her off.

San Geronimo Church, a lovely small brown and white adobe building with twin bell towers, stood at the center of the Pueblo. As the guide told of its history, Rip continued to look back toward the old man's shop. He bumped into a woman trying to take a photo. Tourists arriving in greater numbers suddenly made him feel more exposed. Rip strode inside the church, wanting to complete their task and put the Pueblo behind them. Gale caught up, needing to tell him they had to go back and find the shopkeeper, but the formidable silence of the chapel stopped her. Its bright white plaster walls offset the dark wooden vigas supporting the ceiling, the worn wooden pews, all drew one's focus to the bright blue niches containing depictions of saints and idols at the altar.

They stood quietly for a few moments, Rip hardly seeing any of it as his thoughts raced. A group of tourists entered, filling the small space. Gale tugged Rip toward the door. The tour guide was waiting at the entrance to the courtyard, so Gale led Rip to an empty corner instead.

"I don't know why I went along with this. Do you think Clastier left us a note in there?" Rip asked. "We should be using our time to get deeper into the Eysen or finding a place to hide, not wasting it on this dead priest." Rip pointed to the church. "And even if he had left some kind of message or clue, he was there so long ago; it's surely been painted over or remodeled away by now."

"Oh my God," Gale said, looking back at the twin bell towers. "We're at the wrong church. Clastier never set foot in this building. It wasn't even here when he was."

"What are you talking about?" Rip asked.

"She just told us." Gale pointed to their tour guide. "This church was built around 1850, to replace the one destroyed by the U.S. Army in 1847."

"Of course, the ruins we saw on the way in."

They hurried over to the guide and asked about the history of the church.

"The original church was built in 1619, at another part of the Pueblo, but was destroyed in the 1680 revolt," she explained. "Soon after, another church was constructed at the same site." She pointed north but Pueblo buildings blocked the view. "And, sadly, it was destroyed again in 1847."

"Can we see the ruins?" Gale asked.

"Certainly. Unfortunately, I have to pick up another tour group at the gate, but I'll show you how to get there. It's easy."

A few minutes later, they stood behind a low adobe wall, which stretched around a field of wooden crosses. At the center of the old cemetery, a solitary adobe bell tower rose from the earth as if it was a natural formation – the lone survivor of the 1847 Taos Revolt.

"It stands there like a martyr," Gale said, "like it shares a poetic vision with the mountains."

Rip looked at Gale in a moment of warmth; then went over the wall.

"That's not allowed," Gale began.

"I know, and I'm sorry. Normally, I'm respectful of culture and traditions, but I'm wanted for murder at the moment," he said, as if breaching the cemetery wall was a minor offence. "And if we're looking for something, let's look, and then get the hell out of here."

Gale scanned the area. They were on a deserted edge of the village. She followed, weaving her way through the crowd of crosses. They reached a crumbling wall next to the bell tower, where stacks of more old and weathered crosses in varying sizes lay piled like old wounded soldiers, forgotten and broken. "When the old crosses fall down, they lean them against the ruined church," Gale said. "One hundred and fifty people were slaughtered, when American soldiers attacked this church in 1847."

"I don't know what you think we will find here. If I had time to do a proper excavation, maybe we could piece something together about Clastier. But we don't, and it wouldn't be likely we'd find anything of him because, as you pointed out, there was an awfully bloody battle here in the meantime."

"Rip, take a deep breath. It's not about digging up the past. We need to look at this through Clastier's eyes. This was his world. And his words helped plant the seeds for the revolt that caused this damage."

Rip looked up at the tower, touched its earthen walls, which rightfully should have melted back into the land at least a century earlier, yet miraculously remained. A strange sense of worlds colliding overtook him.

He glanced over at Gale, and was astounded to see her meditating. She sat on the ground, back against the rough wall, inhaling deliberately. Rip's first impulse was to yell at her how inappropriate it was; for a hundred obvious reasons. Instead, for reasons he didn't understand, he joined her.

Rip closed his eyes, and tried to push the knots of tension and fear from his fatigued mind. He felt as if he were naked in front of a crowd and found it difficult to relax. But the warm sun on his face, and the stillness of the Pueblo, quieted his nerves.

Lost in meditation, he heard nothing- until a heavy blow to his chest paralyzed him, and Gale's then piercing scream.

thirteen

Sean Stadler sat behind the wheel of a rental car, in the hotel parking lot. Busman, in the passenger seat, worked the screen of what looked like a custom iPad; while deep in conversation. Sean couldn't hear the other voice, coming through a tiny receiver fitted in Busman's ear. He did know that Rip hadn't been caught yet, but there had been constant calls and data coming in to Busman, who periodically checked his pulse and heart rate on his fitness band.

The other NSA operatives were in two vehicles behind him. They'd all stayed up late last night preparing for this. Busman was meticulous, reminding Sean of his old high school chemistry teacher, only much shorter. "One thing leads to another. Each action creates a reaction. Consequences, that's what we're interested in," the teacher had said, at least once, during every class period that entire year. Sean, not a great student, had pulled a low B in the class; more for his people skills, than his ability as a chemist.

Being likeable came naturally to both Sean and his brother. Sean sensed that Busman liked him too. If he got the chance to see Gale and Rip again, he would need every bit of the Stadler charm to pull off what he needed to do.

How did they expect him to rejoin Rip and act as if nothing had happened? Knowing the NSA would be hearing every word they said. Part of him hoped Rip got caught first, so he wouldn't have to go through with the act. But more than that, Sean wanted a chance to make everything right.

He wished he could talk to his brother about it, wished he could talk to him about anything at all. But this would have been way over Josh's head. Sean had heard enough of Busman's communications during the last forty-eight hours to know this was huge. The National-freakin'-Security Agency was in charge. He'd overheard names he knew from the news – big shots from the White House, Senator Monroe; wasn't he predicted to be the next president? The Pope! It was all a little too "James Bond" for him. But he didn't really care about national security or politics. Sean Stadler had one objective in mind, the only thing that he clung to during the desperate grief he felt over the death of his brother.

When they were kids, Josh used to make monkey sounds and called him "Curious Sean," because Sean's curiosity always seemed to land him in trouble. So much of what had happened since Josh called, asking him to help Gale and Rip, didn't make sense. It made his head hurt, but he kept trying to figure it out; like a jigsaw puzzle, with missing pieces. The Vatican part intrigued him most. He'd taken a Religious Studies course in college because he heard it was easy and filled with pretty girls – neither had been true. But he remembered the time they spent on the history of the Catholic Church, from the crusades to Papal manipulations of European royalty and politics, to the controversial role the Vatican played in World War II. They focused on the seeming epidemic of pedophile priests and subsequent cover-ups. It was no wonder the Church was in decline – its opposition to gays, women rights and birth control seemed out of step with the modern world and the needs of its diverse billion-plus congregation.

Then, one day, it had all changed. For reasons he still didn't understand, and wasn't sure anyone else did either, the sitting Pope resigned. In two thousand years, it had only happened only a handful of times and the last was six hundred years earlier. Sean, like most people who even casually followed the Vatican, found the development very surprising. He wasn't Catholic, but understood the Pope's influence on the world; specifically the 1.6 billion faithful. It seemed encouraging when the new Pope began making great changes to restore the Church to something more than it had become.

The Vatican's involvement in the Gaines case didn't fit the new face of the Church. Sean understood the artifacts might have some religious significance, but he heard things about Vatican agents. Even in his Religious Studies course, they hadn't covered anything about Catholic spies and Church espionage. One thing he had learned was that in the Vatican, the Pope doesn't call all the shots. There is the Curia, Catholicism's Rome-based bureaucracy, and its many secret committees; so it was impossible to know the real villains or motives.

But as he sat in the rental car, waiting for a desperate operation to begin, what worried him most was why he had been allowed to hear so many classified conversations. Busman didn't seem worried that Sean might run to the media once he was free. Sean Stadler knew he was likeable and curious, but he also knew he'd always been considered a bit of an airhead by friends. He clenched the steering wheel tightly; listening to Busman's clipped commands to some faceless technician, probably located thousands of miles away, and tried to think. He had to figure it out. Something was wrong with this picture; he just didn't know what. It was time to get smart, and time was running out.

fourteen

The pain burned through Rip's ribs. Although doubled over, he managed to look up, but just as he focused on the old shopkeeper; another boot slammed into his stomach, and he collapsed again.

"Pick him up," the shopkeeper said to the young man, who had kicked Rip. Another guy held Gale.

"Stop screaming or this will be worse," the young man warned.

"Why are you doing this?" she cried.

"You're on sacred ground," the man holding her growled.

"No," the shopkeeper said, looking into Rip's eyes. "You have been on this ground before; it is for that crime that you must first pay."

"What are you talking about? This is the first time either one of us has visited the Pueblo," Gale said, fighting to break free.

"No," the shopkeeper said sharply. "This one has done great harm here." He pointed a finger into Rip's face and then slapped him.

"Stop it!" Gale screamed.

"What have I done?" Rip asked, gritting his teeth against the pain.

"You came here in search of Clastier," the old man said.

Rip managed to turn toward Gale. Her face registered the same disbelief.

"How did you know?" Gale asked.

"The soul cannot hide. I see him."

"Who? Who do you see?" Gale demanded.

"Conway."

"Who is Conway? That's not his name," Gale said, trying to make sense of the senseless old man. "Are you related to Tagu? Is that how you know about Clastier?"

"I *am* Tagu."

Rip shook his head and sighed. "Tagu has been dead for at least a hundred and fifty years."

"Souls do *not* die. Your ignorance confuses you."

"You're confused, damn it!" Rip yelled.

"Wait," Gale said. "Are you saying you are the reincarnation of Tagu?"

"The soul continues. And Conway must face justice," the shopkeeper said.

"Please," Gale said. "Who was Conway?"

"Conway hunted Clastier, for the Italians."

"So, you didn't mean Rip was searching for Clastier today, you meant back when Clastier was alive?"

The shopkeeper looked confused.

"But he couldn't have been Conway. We're here today trying to save Clastier."

"This is ridiculous," Rip said. "Reincarnation, come on, Gale." He turned to the shopkeeper. "Let us go, now."

The two thugs looked at the shopkeeper.

"Tell me why you came back after so much time, Conway." The shopkeeper spat at Rip.

"I'm not Conway!" Rip growled.

"Grandfather, what are you doing?" the tour guide yelled from the wall.

"Let us be, girl, go away!" He yelled back at her.

She shouted back in their native language of Tewa. Rip couldn't understand but got the meaning. "Listen to her," Rip said. "Let us go." He turned to the man holding Gale. "He's old and senile. I am not Conway. I've never been here before."

"You came here with the troops!" The shopkeeper yelled. "You did this. You killed them. You did!"

"This happened in 1847. My great-great-grandparents weren't even alive then!" Rip tried to break free, but he was no match for the strong Native American man holding him.

"You massacred them because they supported Clastier! You killed my ancestors because they carried Clastier's words."

"No. I have spent my life seeking to *prove* Clastier's words."

"I don't want to hear your lies. I was there. I saw your murdering ways."

"My God, karma can be a brutal thing," Gale said quietly.

"You believe this fairytale?" Rip asked. "What? I was some guy named Conway and led the charge to kill all these innocent people hiding in this church because they supported Clastier? We're talking about Clastier, Gale! My Clastier! Even if I believed in reincarnation, why would I come back more than a century and a half later to risk my life to try to save his words?"

"Karma," Gale said.

"Oh, good God!"

"Rip, you can't deny the situation. He recognized you from another lifetime. A time when you were doing the exact opposite of what you are doing in this life. Don't you see? You're making up for past mistakes."

"Damn it, Gale, look." Rip motioned his head across the cemetery. A Pueblo police car pulled up; two uniformed officers got out and started jogging toward them.

fifteen

Nanski fiddled with his Saint Christopher medal. "That was Pisano. The FBI is in town and they're moving on the Taos Pueblo right now! Let's go."

While Leary drove, Nanski pushed a button on his phone and twenty seconds later a number in Rome rang. "I need to know everything about Clastier."

"Little survived," the Cardinal replied.

"Gaines is at the Taos Pueblo right now. The FBI will likely beat us to him. If I'd known more, we could have anticipated him going there first." Nanski knew the Vatican archives were unsurpassed in their volume and historic depth. More than fifteen centuries before the dawn of the information age, a Pope recognized that information was power. The Vatican knew the world's secrets, and rarely did anyone see all the facets of a secret. "I need everything," he repeated.

"It may take some time."

"I pray we have any time left at all."

On Barbeau's orders, the FBI agents watching the Vatican men, followed at a safe distance. Barbeau knew the Vatican was getting information directly to Attorney General

Dover's office and was determined to keep them under surveillance, even after he captured Gaines.

Pisano was on the phone with the Attorney General at the same time, pushing for Dover's agreement to turn the artifacts over to the Vatican; should the government locate them. Although Dover considered himself a Catholic first, and an American second, as the United States Attorney General; he couldn't just turn over evidence in a criminal proceeding, let alone significant cultural artifacts, to the Vatican. Pisano was asking him to break the law or, as he had put it, "circumvent the law of man to obey the law of God." And Pisano brought tremendous pressure to bear. In the modern era, the Church operated behind the scenes, but its influence and power were greater than ever. Even more than that, they had files . . . on everyone; a database of information on important citizens, high officials, even entire countries. Dover didn't know what to do, but knew either way it would end badly. After the call, he knelt next to his office window and prayed.

Senator Monroe insisted the Attorney General meet with him. The two most visible Catholics in the country met in a secluded park outside Washington, D.C. Each had his own security detail shadowing him as they walked along a maintained, but little used, trail.

"Damn it, this thing has the potential to become a complete disaster!" The Senator said. "It's only a matter of time before the media puts some of the pieces together. Charging such a well-known figure with murder . . . what the hell were you thinking?" He snapped his fingers and pointed at Dover, as if commanding an answer.

Dover, although well aware of the Senator's odd habit of snapping his fingers, still took offense. "Aren't you afraid that your affair with his accomplice, Gale Asher, will become a scandal?"

The Senator, having been in politics too long, hid his surprise that Dover knew about something so far in his past. "It's got nothing to do with her."

"I think your Christian constituency might disagree, especially when your 'friends' in the liberal media get wind of it."

Monroe laughed. "You're a slippery bastard, Dover. Maybe you're just jealous because I get laid a lot more than you do, or you just want to take the attention off your many mistakes in handling this case. I thought you were trying to keep the media at bay, yet you indicted a celebrity. Christ, Gaines has got a million Twitter followers. Even more, since you made him 'America's most wanted professor.' And you think me doing a beautiful college student thirteen years ago is news? You're trying to cover up your own mess."

"We needed some help in getting him off the streets."

"So you're desperate?" the Senator asked, gruffly.

"I'm not the one running for president."

"Oh, aren't you?"

"You know, I've not announced my intentions."

"Ha!"

Dover smiled. "Perhaps if I do, you could be my running mate. You have the look of a vice president. Although an affair with a criminal . . . those things have been known to derail campaigns."

"You're a little too obsessed with my love life. Have you spent too much time staring at Gale Asher's photos?

Do you want me to fix you up with her? Is that it?" The Senator snapped three times, alternating hands.

"She was your student, Senator. You're still friends and now she is wanted as an accessory to murder, theft of government property, aiding and abetting, et cetera. When was the last time you spoke to her?"

"None of your damn business. You know none of that garbage will stick to me. I'm the next president of the United States."

"We'll see what the election brings."

"Election?" he said, as if the word was new to him. "The election is theatre; my rise to the presidency is preordained."

"By God?"

"Yes, by Him. And more importantly, by the people who actually make these decisions." He snapped both hands and twirled his index fingers.

Dover didn't like Monroe's brand of faith, but the truth was that they were old friends; the kind for which the term "frenemies" was coined. And Dover had long known he didn't stand a chance against Senator Monroe in the primaries. But this explosive case contained enough traps, landmines, and tripwires that anything could happen. It could destroy them both or land one of them in the White House.

"Have you had a visit from Pisano?" Dover asked.

"That pushy little weasel is the reason we needed to meet." The Senator stopped walking. "Listen, Harry, let's find a way to give them the artifacts. Whatever they are, we don't care and we don't have any use for them. It could be a chunk of the cross, or the Ark of the Covenant, for all it matters to us. Let's keep Rome happy."

"What do they have on you, Senator?"

"Nothing, except maybe the keys to eternal salvation. My church needs my help."

"What about your country?"

"My country doesn't need a few dusty objects; dug up in the Virginia mountains. My country needs a strong relationship with the Vatican."

"And if I were willing, which I'm not saying I am, how do you suggest I go about it?"

"That's not my area. They get 'destroyed' in the arrest, lost in storage, sent for study, and misplaced in shipment; it's happened before. You'll come up with something."

"Why is it my hands that have to get dirty?" Dover asked.

"Because I'm the next president." The Senator slapped Dover's back and laughed. Dover didn't think it was funny.

"What if I told you that we're not the only ones who want those artifacts?" Dover asked.

"As long as it isn't the Chinese or the Russians, I'm not too worried about it," the Senator said. "Don't tell me National Geographic has called you."

"How about your friends at the National Security Agency?"

"You're not serious!" He stopped again and stared at Dover. "They called you?"

"No, they're operating around us."

"Damn it, that's even worse."

sixteen

The two men holding Gale and Rip were unsure what to do when they saw the Pueblo cops coming. Fearing they could be arrested for assaulting tourists, they released their grip. Without hesitation, Gale and Rip bolted.

The shopkeeper gave chase, but tripped and became tangled in the crosses. One officer reached the two Indians, who were helping the shopkeeper to his feet. The other patrolman ran to intersect Gale and Rip, now separated as they dashed through the cemetery.

Rip hurtled the far wall, not realizing the ground on the other side was much lower. He sacrificed his knee in order to avoid his backpack with the Eysen, taking the brunt of the fall. Landing in a parking lot outside the village, he sprang to his feet, ignoring the pain and blood.

Rip spotted an older heavy-set couple in leather jumpsuits; who had just gotten off a wide Harley. The keys, still in the ignition, were too tempting; he pushed the man out of the way, unintentionally sending him crashing to the ground. The woman screamed and went to her husband's aid, as Rip jumped on the bike.

Gale emerged from behind a building forty feet ahead; he slowed just enough to allow her to climb on, then sped away.

"You're full of surprises, professor," Gale shouted over the engine's roar.

"I had a Harley all through college."

While winding up Miller Road, Rip kept checking the side mirror. He felt bad about pushing that man down, but if he'd been caught, death was certain. The narrow road dead-ended into Spider Road, and after a quick turn; led them back to Paseo Del Pueblo Norte, the main drag and away from the Pueblo.

"Get off the main road," Gale yelled in his ear. He hung a left onto Kit Carson Road and found his way onto the back streets.

"No one seems to be after us. Let's go to San Francisco de Asís Church," Gail said, grasping her hat so it wouldn't blow off.

"Hell no! We're leaving town."

"It's on the way." Her hair whipped in the wind.

"Damn it, Gale, you're crazy!" Rip coughed as a bug shot down his throat at fifty miles per hour.

"Pull over!" she shouted.

"I want out of Taos," he said, as they stopped in front of a parked car.

"Are you running from the FBI or from Conway?"

"Both!"

"You have to admit it's pretty amazing that the shopkeeper knew Clastier."

"He didn't know Clastier. He knows some obscure history. He's delusional."

"Fine, forget about reincarnation. He still picked you out as connected to Clastier. How do you explain that?"

"I don't have to, I don't care."

"Yes, you do."

"Sure it's weird, I don't deny that, but I've got a black crystal ball in my pack that has kind of numbed me to weird."

"We can't drive a stolen motorcycle forever. We're going to have to get off the road. Please, just go to the church."

"You want to seek sanctuary in a church? How fitting."

"I just want five minutes."

"Then where?"

"I don't know."

"You don't know why you want to go to the church either. Clastier didn't leave a note for us at the last one."

"Didn't he?"

"I didn't see one!" Rip said, exasperated.

"Clastier sure found a way to communicate with us at the Pueblo church."

"A freak coincidence," he yelled, not believing his own words. "Fine, we'll go, but then I'm calling Booker. It's not just time to leave Taos; it's time to get out of the country."

A few minutes later they arrived at San Francisco de Asís Mission Church. Instead of stopping, Rip drove to the next street and pulled the bike into a narrow row of trees.

"It's not too hard to see," Gale said, pointing to the large shiny motorcycle.

"I don't see anywhere better."

Gale broke off a few branches and tried to cover the license plate.

"Let's just get this over with," Rip said. He saw a place across the street that might have a payphone.

Rip couldn't help but be struck by the beauty of the church, its smooth, round, earthen walls, and massive adobe buttresses. "It's been photographed by Ansel Adams and painted by Georgia O'Keefe," Gale said.

They hurried inside. A bearded Hispanic man was answering questions from a group of high school kids. Rip had noticed the bus in the parking lot. "Yes, construction began in 1776, and it's been in continuous use ever since its completion around 1810, although some of us historians argue about the dates," the man said.

Rip scanned the ornate, colorful altar that filled the back of the church. The high white walls rose to a crown of hand-hewn vigas. He saw no messages from Clastier and, more importantly, no angry old shopkeepers with poison in their eyes.

"Did a priest named Clastier ever preach within these walls?"

The question startled Rip, even though he recognized Gale's voice; he didn't quite believe she was sharing a secret so publicly. The historian apparently agreed. He squinted his eyes at Gale and couldn't seem to find his voice. Rip searched for a place to become invisible.

"I think that's all we have time for today," the historian finally said, nodding to the class's teacher, who took the hint and worked at corralling her students.

"Maybe you'd like to speak outside," the historian said, stepping close to Gale. They walked to the door as students were flooding out. Rip reluctantly followed.

"I'm sorry, but would you please repeat your question," the historian asked, looking at Rip suspiciously.

"I want to know about Clastier," Gale said.

"I'm sorry but it is forbidden."

"Forbidden? By who?" Rip asked.

"By Papal decree."

seventeen

Nanski and Leary reached the Pueblo, unknowingly trailed by an entourage of FBI agents, less than ten minutes after Barbeau and Hall arrived.

Barbeau was still trying to navigate the unusual bureaucracy of the sovereign nation, while Hall was discussing the matter with the war chief. Nothing could be done until the tribal governor arrived. Two other agents were trying to find the officer involved in the event. No one seemed to know what happened.

Nanski and Leary made the same mistake Gale and Rip had, by going to the "new" San Geronimo church.

"There's no one here," Nanski said. "Maybe the feds already have them."

"What about that old church tower?" Leary asked. He'd read tourism pamphlets during his hours staking out San Francisco de Asís.

"Show me," Nanski said. They sprinted through a short maze of Pueblo buildings and found the empty police cruiser parked near the cemetery entrance. The shopkeeper and his helpers had already been cleared off, but Nanski spotted another Pueblo police vehicle in a parking area beyond the wall. As they ran through the cemetery, Leary

crossed himself in the traditional *signum crucis* and recited
the trinitarian formula.

After dropping off the wall into the parking area,
Leary pointed to a rescue squad. A paramedic was tending
to an older man dressed in a leather jumpsuit, while his
wife hovered over him. In that instant, Nanski felt deflated.
Was this the incident that had brought them here? Was this
the couple police were seeking? Had Gaines even been
here? He went over to the EMT, and sent Leary to the
police officer.

The EMT knew nothing, but the woman was happy to
provide details.

"Oh, a crazy man came flying over that wall there and
shoved my husband to the ground. Stole our Harley! He
nearly killed us both!"

"I'm so sorry this happened to you, ma'am. You could
help us catch him, if you could tell us what he looked like."

"Well, of course, I already told the police, but it
happened so fast. He was a blur, but I do remember he had
a backpack."

"Could you tell me your license plate number?"

"I gave it to the other officer. Are you a detective?"

"Something, like that. I'm afraid you may be asked to
tell your story a few more times. It's important to help
capture this thug."

"Yes, he is a thug," she agreed, and gave him the plate
number.

"Thank you. I'm sure your husband will be fine."
Nanski saw the man only had a few scrapes, maybe a
bruised ego; mostly it had just been traumatic. "God bless
you," he said, and walking away, immediately made a
phone call.

Busman's NSA subordinate had urged him to get to the Pueblo. Instead, he insisted they all head south. "The flare up at the Pueblo will force them out of town and the most logical route is right past here," he said, pulling into the parking lot of the Sagebrush Inn. "We've got a good view of the highway and listening to the Police band, we'll find out more."

"The FBI will make the arrest," the junior agent repeated.

"Hold tight. We're fine right here." Busman turned to Sean "Are you ready? You know what to do?"

"I think so," Sean stuttered.

While they waited, Busman finished his daily jog that had been interrupted earlier. As he did laps around the large parking lot, he thought of his model-beautiful wife. If all went well, he'd be back home in a couple of days.

Barbeau and Hall were hung up so long with the war chief that, by the time they reached the parking lot where Rip had taken the motorcycle, Nanski and Leary were already gone. They thought it best to head back into town and hoped the Town of Taos Police would spot the stolen motorcycle. The Pueblo cop had told Nanski that the state police were working with the FBI and that agents were already at the Pueblo. The multi-jurisdictional case was going to be a mess.

Hall talked to the woman and showed her a photo of Gaines. She was positive that he was the thief. Oddly, she hadn't seen Gale, but the Pueblo police confirmed she had been with him earlier. They were still searching the reservation for her.

"Do you think she's still hiding here?" Barbeau asked an officer.

"We're searching, sir, but the Pueblo is ninety-nine thousand acres stretching into the mountains. She may have made it to the edge of town by now. Could be anywhere."

Barbeau scanned the hills. "If they're still separated, we may have just caught a break."

"Let's get a bird in the sky," Hall said.

"Let's get a few," Barbeau said, as his phone rang.

Hall called in a request for air surveillance. It would take thirty-five minutes.

"What the hell?" Barbeau said, hanging up. "Screw Dover!"

"What now?" Hall asked.

"The Justice Department just withdrew the murder charges for Gaines."

"Wow, that's a surprise."

"Not only that, they cancelled all arrest warrants on him."

"You mean, now he's not even wanted for theft of government property?"

"I mean, he's not even wanted for assaulting Senior Knievel over there."

"So we're not on the case anymore?"

eighteen

The teenagers were swarming around the San Francisco de Asís Mission Church taking pictures, laughing and generally creating a hectic backdrop to the intense conversation Gale and Rip were having with the historian.

"What does that mean? A Papal decree that we can't talk about Clastier?"

"It means that he never existed."

"The Pope can do that? Wipe out a man's entire lifetime? Erase him from history?" Rip was incredulous.

"Of course, it would be almost impossible to do that today, but the world was quite different in the nineteenth century. His disappearance predates the 1847 Pueblo Revolt; the Church wielded tremendous power, as they do today. The difference is there were no computers, or telephones; even books were scarce. Most people, even the one you speak of, left little trace in the world, and what trace he did leave could very easily be expunged by the powerful."

"Why are you afraid to say his name?" Rip challenged.

"I don't even know your name. Why would I defy my church to satisfy a stranger?"

"My name is Gale Asher." She held out her hand. Rip could not believe she was using her real name.

The historian shook her hand. "I am Fernando Martinez Aragón. And your eyes exceed the beauty of the wondrous blue topaz in Queen Isabella's crown jewels. You must be a descendent of fairies."

Rip shook his head, even though the description fit what he considered the most captivating eyes he'd ever seen. "My name is Conway," Rip said abruptly.

Gale couldn't help but cough. "Please, Mr. Aragón, we need to know about Clastier," she said.

"His life did not happen."

"You have no idea what we've been through to get this far."

"I'm sorry, but as I said, the man you seek never existed." The historian looked at Rip. "Do you exist, Mr. Conway?"

Rip stared back at the historian. Gale looked pleadingly at both of them. "My name isn't Conway. I'm Professor Ripley Gaines."

"Of course you are," the historian said. "I've seen you interviewed many times; read about your digs with great interest. And now all this terrible business."

"I swear we didn't kill anyone," Gale said.

"Apparently not. As I pulled into the parking lot, the news reported all charges had been dropped."

"What?" Rip asked, shocked. "Are you sure?"

"Quite."

Gale hugged Rip.

"Hugs all around," the historian said, cutting in on Rip as if they were all on a dance floor. "I must admit it would have made for a better story to tell my students that I helped a murderer escape justice. Oh well, I'll just have to embellish a little here and there; we occasionally do that with history."

"We need to know about Clastier," Gale asked again.

"I cannot help you; my apologies, sweet lady. He did not exist."

"How can you call yourself a historian?" Rip asked.

"If he didn't exist, then what are these?" Gale said, taking the papers out of her backpack.

"Not here, Gale." Rip tried to grab the papers, but Gale held them away.

"Why not? He needs to believe us."

"Those papers aren't yours," Rip said to Gale, as she handed them to the historian. "We don't know this man. Why do we care what he believes?"

"Because he knows something of Clastier, and we need to know all we can."

The historian stared disbelievingly at the documents in his hands. "My God, *los papeles que faltan. . . Son verdaderos*," he whispered.

"What did he say?" Rip asked.

"He said, 'the missing papers, they are real.' Please, tell us what you know about Clastier," Gail begged the historian.

The historian stared into her eyes and finally spoke. "I cannot . . . but perhaps someone else can. Do you know El Santuario de Chimayó?"

"Yes, the church?"

"Right. There is an old woman who lives very near the church. Her family home predates the chapel. She knows of whom you speak." He sifted through the papers, looking longingly at them. "Are they real?"

"Yes." Gale nodded.

"Are they incredible?" the historian asked; his voice and expression conveyed a combination of sadness, hope, and awe.

"Yes," she said, reaching for the papers. "Breathtakingly so."

He handed the pages back to her without leaving her eyes. Only when she broke their gaze did the historian turn his attention back to Rip. "I'll call Teresa and tell her to expect you." He pulled out his business card and wrote down the old woman's name, address, and telephone number. "Find the church; her house is on the street before."

"If you won't even speak his name, how do you know she has information?" Rip asked.

"Teresa has more than information. I am a well-known historian, perhaps the leading authority on northern New Mexico. I'm also a Church historian. The two are so very intertwined, you know? She came to me many years ago with her questions, her mystery . . . and something else."

"What else?" Rip asked.

"Ah, that is not my story to tell."

"Why didn't you just ask to use his cell phone?" Gale asked Rip, after the historian had driven off.

"I don't want Booker's number on a stranger's phone."

"Do you still consider the historian a stranger? He knows of Clastier."

"So does the Pope and we're not exactly close. Come on, this town is so old, there's bound to be a payphone around; it might even cost only a dime."

"Look," Gale said, alarmed, pointing through the trees to where they left the stolen motorcycle. Rip saw the state trooper standing next to it, talking on the radio.

"Damn, we're off the hook for murder, but now I'm wanted for assault and grand theft! He hasn't seen us, let's go." They ran north and cut through a dusty plaza; emerging in the parking lot of the Ranchos de Taos Post Office.

Suddenly a car turned off Paseo del Pueblo onto San Francisco Road and stopped in front of them. The window rolled down and the driver yelled, "Gale, Rip, I can't believe I found you!"

nineteen

Nanski and Leary missed Gale and Rip by minutes. The FBI converged on the San Francisco de Asís Church soon after. The teenagers, their teacher, and the historian were already gone, but they would be found and questioned later.

Barbeau and Hall returned to the state police headquarters. They were in limbo since no federal charges were pending against Gaines. The Director was working on it. In the meantime, the field agents were trying to track down witnesses and footage from traffic cameras that might have picked up Gale and Rip's movements. A team from the Pueblo was still canvassing the area for Gale.

"I just can't figure out why the Attorney General dropped all the charges against Gaines," Hall said. He'd asked the question several times since they got the news and he didn't like Barbeau's theory.

"I keep telling you, we were getting too close. He wants the Vatican to get him first so they can kill him," Barbeau repeated, impatiently.

"I don't think so. He could have pulled us at anytime."

"We'll see what the Director says."

"I think someone asked Dover to drop the charges, or . . . told him to do it."

"Told him? Only one person can tell the Attorney General to drop charges. Are you saying the President of the United States is interfering with a federal murder investigation?"

"Maybe. But maybe someone else has the juice to get Dover to act."

"The Pope?"

"Clearly. Dover has been acting at the Vatican's behest all along, so the charges probably would never have been filed without their approval."

"Gaines could not have killed Ian Sweedler. Perhaps, the Attorney General finally figured that out and backed out of the mistake as quickly as possible."

"I've thought of that, but one, he likely knew all along the murder rap was bogus; two, why drop all charges, including theft; and three, the timing of the dismissal was extraordinary – we practically had Gaines."

"Then who?"

"Booker Lipton, Senator Monroe, the President, or someone as yet unknown to us."

"I'll give it to the Director, when he calls. DIRT is already working on backgrounds and case connections for all of them. But I'll tell him your theory and we'll see if he thinks it flies."

"One of the field agents just sent me a text. Three witnesses have confirmed Gale Asher was with Gaines at San Francisco de Asís. Better call off the Pueblo search."

"Funny. Remember how some of the students at the dig site said he was furious she was there? I guess they've grown closer over the past week."

"If Booker Lipton asked Dover to drop the charges, wouldn't Gaines have known? He sure acted like a desperate man this morning, and is, by all indications, still running like a frightened fugitive."

"Running is the key word. We've got the motorcycle and no other vehicles have been reported stolen, the Vatican guys are accounted for, so where the hell are they? How did they get out of there?"

Booker was on the grounds of a mansion overlooking the Potomac River just outside Washington, D.C., when Kruse phoned him. The estate belonged to a friend and was occasionally used by Booker for sensitive meetings with government officials.

"I was just calling you. Anything?" Booker asked.

"We've got nothing," Kruse said, while loading an HK MK23 handgun to supplement his Glock-19. "They narrowly escaped the Taos Pueblo Police and now have disappeared once again. The feds are at San Fran –"

Booker cut him off. "I know about the morning events. It's laughable that the Bureau is having such trouble apprehending Gaines, but I'm not amused that you can't get him either. This may be our last shot; now go to this address in Chimayó; you should find him there. If he resists, take whatever non-lethal means are necessary. "

Booker hung up, popped two ashwaganda pills for stress, and took a swig of apple/carrot juice from his flask, then walked back inside and apologized to Senator Monroe.

"Forgive me, Senator, I had to take that. Messy matter in China."

"Aren't they always," the Senator joked, snapping his fingers three times as if adding a "ba-dum-bump" to his punch line.

"Senator, do you really want to be president?" Booker asked. "There are pressures you can't imagine, even if you think you can; the constant threat of assassination, and never-ending attacks from the opposing party; trying to destroy your fragile reputation, and engulf you in a scandal that is new and exciting enough to shock a nearly unshockable nation. And for what? It isn't the salary; I pay corporate vice presidents ten times as much. The ego boost? They may claim the president is the most powerful person on earth, but his power is a fraction of mine, and I'm not even top dog; not to mention, I don't have to get re-elected. So all that risk for four, maybe eight years' worth of surface power, low pay, and average benefits. Hell, it can't be Air Force One; I could give you a much nicer plane than that."

"Booker, you make it sound so appealing." The senator laughed, setting down his wine. "It's more about history."

"Ah, yes, the legacy; the exclusive club of presidents in the history books. All the better if you take us into a war. Wartime presidents are generally regarded higher in public opinion polls; historians give them bonus points for navigating a war, even unsuccessful ones."

"I'll keep that in mind."

"Senator, the kind of favorable history you're looking for can take fifty years to hit the books, and hell, it isn't even real. I'll give you one billion dollars to do with whatever you want, buy a bunch of gumballs for all I care. One billion dollars ought to pay for plenty of history books."

"You want me to withdraw from the race?"

"I don't really care about that, but if I give you a billion dollars; you'd probably have to. You can't hide that kind of gift. Believe me, I've tried. No, what I want for a billion dollars is for you to turn your back on something more important to you than the presidency of the United States."

twenty

Sean Stadler leaned out the car window and smiled. "Need a lift?"

"I don't believe it!" Gale squealed.

"What the hell are you doing here?" Rip shouted.

"Jump in, I'll explain everything. I can't believe I really found you."

Rip got in front and Gale climbed in the back. She immediately wrapped her arms around him from behind and kissed his cheek. "How *did* you find us?"

"Would you mind driving while you talk?" Rip asked. "I think it's best we get far away from Taos as quickly as possible."

"No problem. It seems like I'm always driving you guys out of trouble." Sean laughed. "Where are we heading?"

"The Interstate," Rip said.

"Closest one is in Santa Fe," Sean said.

"Take the back roads; 518 isn't far," Gale said, folding a map she'd picked up at the motel. We need to make a stop in Chimayó."

"No," Rip said. "We're not making that mistake again."

"It's not a mistake," Gale said.

"We found nothing at the last church."

"How can you say that? We found the historian."

"I suppose you think Clastier sent him?"

"He knew Clastier."

"Come on, Gale, he said he didn't exist."

"You know that's not what he said."

"Are you trying to get us arrested? We need to get somewhere safe, somewhere we can study what's really important." He looked back at Gale. "If you want to know what Clastier would tell you to do right now, he'd say, 'forget about me, study what I told you to look for,' and you know it." He arched his eyebrow for emphasis before turning back to Sean. "So, if you don't mind turning around up here and heading to Santa Fe . . . "

"It's safer for us to go the back way," Gale pleaded, "and we'll be in Santa Fe a couple of hours later. This is the last church, I promise."

"No."

"Then let me out."

"Guys, guys, wow. I leave you alone for a few days and you wind up fighting like an old married couple. Now come on, Rip, she sounds reasonable."

"Look, Sean, you have no idea what she sounds like after all we've been through. You're not really part of this so why – "

Sean jammed on the brakes, swerving into the parking lot of an old woodworking shop. Rip, who hadn't buckled up, slammed into the dash. The pack in his lap helped cushion the blow but he still hit his head on the windshield.

"Hey, what the hell!" Rip yelled. Gale was strapped in, in the back and fine.

"I'll apologize right after you." Sean glared at Rip.

"What do I have to apologize for?"

"For saying I'm not really part of this," Sean blasted. "Excuse the hell out of me, did your brother get killed because of this?" His voice broke as he yelled. "The FBI is after me, they've harassed my grieving parents. I've twice driven you out of harm's way, crossed the whole damn country hoping to find you, and you have the gall to tell me I'm not part of this? My brother is dead, you arrogant bastard!"

"I'm sorry, Sean, I truly am. You're right; I'm an arrogant bastard. I never stop thinking about Josh. I'm so sorry." His eyes filled with tears. "You have no idea how sorry I am."

"He is, Sean. We talk about Josh all the time. I miss him," Gale said, sadly. She put her hands on his shoulders.

"I know," Sean said. "Me too." He put the car into gear and pulled into traffic. "You all right?" he asked.

"Yeah," Rip said.

"Sorry about that," Sean said. "You should put on your seatbelt."

Rip nodded, buckling the belt.

"Chimayó then?" Sean asked.

"I guess so," Rip sighed.

"Thanks," Gale said from the backseat. Rip didn't know if she was thanking him or Sean, so he didn't respond.

After a few miles of silence Gale spoke. "So tell us the story. How did you wind up in Taos?"

Sean told them about the call from someone warning him to get out of Josh's house before the cops got there, the agony of telling his parents about Josh's death, the FBI coming to the door, and his run to the bus station. It was a long story; forty-five minutes of rolling northern New

Mexico countryside passed as they traveled what locals called the High Road. They were just outside of Ojo Sarco, about twenty minutes away from Chimayó, when Sean's story began to deviate from the truth.

"Once I knew the FBI was after me, I got to my cousin's place in Greensboro and he rented this car for me. Then I headed straight to Asheville, where I was hoping to meet up with you guys again. I didn't know where else to go or what else to do."

"How were you going to find us?" Gale asked.

"Rip had given me a phone number and said the person could get a message to you."

"I gave him Booker's number," Rip told Gale.

"Yeah, but as it turned out," Sean continued, "I lost that scrap of paper somewhere. It didn't matter because when I got to Asheville, I didn't stay because the place was swarming with feds. A college buddy who graduated last year lives in Memphis; I figured it was as good a place to hide as any. But it was crazy; when I got there we just had time for a quick drink before a family emergency had him heading to Dallas. We caravanned for a while, because I didn't know where to go. I was in Oklahoma, when I heard about the murder charge, which I knew was a crock. The news said you were believed to be in the Taos area; there'd been some big raid. I headed straight here. Can you believe it? I was like a mile away when I heard on the radio that the murder charges were dropped, but local police were still after you for questioning over a stolen bike that had just been spotted at San Francisco de Asís.

"It's fate," Gale said.

"What?" Sean asked.

"That you found us again," Gale answered.

"Gale probably thinks a dead priest sent you to us," Rip said, sarcastically.

"I wouldn't doubt it," she said.

twenty-one

They found the old lady's house, a small adobe shaded in trees. The wispy and small woman appeared frail, and might have been eighty, possibly even ninety. "What do you want?" she said in her toughest voice, which was too raspy to scare anyone.

"Are you Teresa? The historian sent us. He said he'd call. My name is Ripley."

"Who are these two?" Teresa waved a bony hand at Gale and Sean. "A couple of vagabonds it looks like."

"No. I'm sorry, they are Gale and Sean, friends of mine," Rip said.

Gale stepped forward and offered her hand. "Nice to meet you ma'am. May we come in?"

Teresa recoiled, almost disappearing in her floral housecoat. "All of you!? My goodness, no. You vagrants can stay in the yard. I'll have tea with Mr. Ripley."

"Teresa, may I call you Teresa?" Rip asked, bowing slightly.

She smiled at him.

"I'd like it if my friends could join us."

"No, no, no. The likes of them can't be trusted." She grabbed a broom and shook it at Sean. "You, boy, watch you don't trample my petunias."

Sean cowered backwards and in his nervousness actually did step on some of the purple flowers. Teresa looked horrified, as if he'd produced a gun. Rip motioned to Gale that they should all just leave, and tried to convey with his eyes that the old lady might be a bit off.

"Rip, you go ahead and talk to Teresa alone. We'll wait out here," Gale said.

"Away from my petunias!" Teresa shouted.

"You're sure?" Rip asked Gale.

She nodded. "Go ahead."

Rip leaned in close to Gale and whispered, "Okay, if I'm not back in an hour, send help."

Gale laughed, which made the old woman trust her even less.

Rip followed Teresa inside. She bolted the lock behind her.

"Have a seat, Mr. Ripley." She pointed to an antique burgundy-colored chair that belonged more in a colonial museum than a southwestern adobe. "I'll bring us some warm tea." While waiting, he looked at portraits adorning the walls, presumably of her ancestors stretching back to the conquistadors. He wondered why he'd agreed to this waste of time.

"Teresa, please don't think me rude, but we're in a bit of a hurry."

"In New Mexico?" She laughed as she came in with a tray of tea. "We have a saying here, *mañana*."

"Yes, it means tomorrow," Rip said.

"Maybe in the rest of the world, but in New Mexico, mañana doesn't mean tomorrow, it means not necessarily today. Time is different here."

Rip smiled and sipped his tea. "Could you tell me what you know about Clastier?"

She stared at him, the wrinkles around her foggy eyes tightened. "It sounds so good to hear a man say that name. Would you mind saying it again?" Her eyes closed.

"Clastier."

She took a long deep breath before speaking. "He never existed . . . do you believe that, Mr. Ripley? Clastier never existed."

"I am certain he existed," Rip said.

"Of course he did! You know he slept in this very house." Her eyes were wide, studying Rip to gauge if her words were shocking enough.

"Really? Did he live here?"

"For a time. Clastier and my thrice-great-grandmother were lovers."

This time Rip's shock was real.

"How do you know?"

"I have their letters."

"You have letters written by Clastier?"

She nodded, proudly.

"May I see them?"

"You cannot have them."

"No, of course not, but could I just look at them?"

"I don't want that shiftless pair you came with knowing about them."

"Certainly not."

She left the room for a couple of minutes and returned with a stack of folded, yellowed paper, tied in worn black twine, almost three inches thick. He looked up for approval as he held the end of the bow. Teresa nodded and smiled.

He immediately recognized Clastier's neat script. Although he couldn't speak Spanish very well, he could read it. He'd started teaching himself the language using Clastier's papers, and the English translations during his youthful summers in North Carolina. The papers didn't just inspire his pursuit of archaeology; they also prompted him to take Spanish in high school and college. "You can't expect to really see the world if you only do it in English," he'd always said. Perusing the letters, he feared might be snatched out of his hands at any moment by the neurotic old woman, he found mention of spiritual ideas, radical at the time, such as reincarnation, a collective consciousness, and even physical and mental powers of the soul, which he recognized in more refined passages from the Attestations section of Clastier's papers. It was exciting to see the rawness of his words, and for the first time, Rip felt a true closeness to the man who had guided so much of his life. It was as if he were reading the private thoughts of a dear old friend. After a long passage about miraculous healings at the Chimayó Church, he knew he'd have to take the letters with him.

twenty-two

The Director explained to Barbeau that, although the Attorney General had dismissed the criminal indictment against Gaines, they still wanted him as a material witness for questioning in multiple crimes, including two murders. Furthermore, the government intended to secure the return of government property, namely the artifacts, "by all available means."

"So nothing has changed?" Hall asked.

"The Director believes Dover dropped the charges in an effort to get rid of all the heat from the state and local jurisdictions that were getting involved. They were impossible to control. The media, although easier to manage, was also becoming a problem."

"So if we capture Gaines . . . ?"

"The Director's best guess goes like this: Department of Justice questions Gaines; the artifacts will disappear either to Rome, or into some bottomless government warehouse, meaning the U.S. intelligence community. Then, within a couple of days, Gaines leaves a tidy note, citing his destroyed reputation, and kills himself."

"I've seen that movie before."

"Yeah, they keep doing remakes of it in Washington, and even though the public knows the ending, they keep buying tickets."

Gale and Sean sat talking in the car in front of the old lady's house. Chimayó, an oasis in northern New Mexico's high desert badlands, seemed mainly covered with large cottonwoods and willows that shielded them from the hot sun.

"She's loony, don't you think?" Sean asked.

"You mean Teresa? She's just old," Gale said. "I don't think she likes strangers."

"She seemed to like Rip."

"Yes, she's from a time and culture where men were respected just because they were men, regardless of their actions."

"Do you respect Rip?" Sean asked.

"That's a funny question."

"Do you?"

"Yes, very much," Gale answered, squinting her eyes.

"Me, too."

"Don't you think your parents are worried about you?"

"Yeah."

"Maybe we can figure out a way to get word to them. Losing Josh, the FBI after you, they're probably going crazy."

"Where are we going next?" Sean changed the subject.

"We're going to need to stop somewhere and buy camping gear. Rip wants to get out of the state, so we'll head west as far as we can go, until we need to sleep."

"Arizona?"

"Initially."

"I can drive all night, or we can take turns. I don't care about this rental; like I did my Jeep."

"Driving late at night means there are fewer vehicles to blend in with and the road is mostly filled with cops and drunks. It's too risky," Rip said.

"Think you'll ever get the Jeep back?" Gale asked.

Sean thought about the good times he'd had in his adored car, about his girlfriend, who had probably been harassed by the FBI, and his brother's final suffering minutes, which he'd imagined a hundred different ways. "It doesn't matter."

Nanski hung up the phone and told Leary, "Punch Chimayó, New Mexico, into the GPS. Gaines is there."

"How do we know this?" Leary asked.

"The Cardinal just told me that Clastier was the priest at Chimayó."

"And if there's no record of that, then how would Gaines know?"

"I'm afraid Gaines has access to better information than the Vatican has."

"That can't be possible. He's just one guy. Surely, he's nothing against the resources of the world's greatest religion, more than a billion and a half Catholics and the Kingdom of Almighty God."

"So far, Gaines has done pretty well for a man who should have been dead a week ago. We'd do well to recall the words of Archimedes, 'Give me a lever long enough, and a fulcrum on which to place it, and I shall move the world.' Gaines has the lever; pray we stop him before he locates the fulcrum."

twenty-three

Rip's hand trembled slightly as he held the nearly two-hundred-year-old letter from Clastier. He read the line for a third time to make sure he was getting the translation correct. *"A black sphere cradled within stone bowls found at Chimayó has made more of an impact on me than anything produced by the Church. Yes, it even rivals the creations of God in its wonder, and grants more into the ways of its secrets; revealing a past so great that one must believe more in God, but far different from the God that Catholicism presents. It is too much to comprehend and yet, it is simple. The pain this tiny glowing planet causes me could not be healed with every medicine known to man, for it is without a doubt that the Church is false. Mistaken at best, fraudulent at worse, and I have helped to perpetuate this lie. And now, they will do what they always do in any disagreement with any dissenter. I will be labeled as a collaborator with the devil, a heretic, and then they will banish or kill me. But my dear sweet Flora, I cannot deny what I have seen and what I know."* Rip leaned back in the old leather barrel chair and closed his eyes.

"Are you okay?" Teresa asked. She touched his arm; her hand felt like warm crepe paper. He opened his eyes and focused on her thin grey hair, trying to rein in his runaway thoughts. Clastier's papers were based on knowledge, at least in part, that he'd gained from an Eysen. Was it the same one concealed within the pack on his back? Impossible! He'd seen that one pulled from an eleven-million-year-old cliff two thousand miles away from where he now sat.

"Do you know what he is talking about here?" Rip pointed to the passage.

"Oh, yes," Teresa said, barely glancing at it.

"Does he say more about it?"

"Oh my, yes."

"Would you allow me to take these letters? I'd like to make copies and study them further."

"Mr. Ripley, I could never part with these."

"It's just that they are possibly . . . I mean, these letters could save my life, could save many lives." Rip was desperate. He didn't feel safe enough to stay there for the hours it would require to read them, but he believed they were the key to his survival. Clastier had had an Eysen! The ramifications overwhelmed him. He considered just dashing out of the house and speeding away. But she would likely call the police, plus he didn't like the idea of becoming a serial artifact thief. "How can I convince you?"

"Mr. Ripley, I could just give you copies."

"You have copies?"

"I made them for the historian. He refused to take them." She made a sour face. "He's a very smart man, but he's too Catholic for this business." Teresa went to an old desk, fiddled with a tiny key and produced a manila envelope. "Clastier was destroyed by the Church, my family was forever changed, but what they took from the world is the greatest crime ever committed," she said, handing the copies to Rip.

"And what did they take?" Rip asked.

She looked at him as though he'd just asked her what year it was. "They took the truth, Mr. Ripley. They stole everything that is real and gave us this," she waved her hands toward the window as if to indicate the outside world, "this mistake!"

"How do you know? Does Clastier say what happened to his sphere?"

"He didn't know what happened to it."

Rip stared, his expression begging her to continue.

"Clastier was gone. The story came down through my family. Clastier had already fled. No one knew if he was in hiding, captured, or dead. The Pope himself ordered the Chimayó Church to be destroyed. They knew he had hidden something, but couldn't find it. It was good fortune they didn't know of his relationship with Flora or this house would have been gone."

"But they didn't destroy the church."

"No, because they found what they were looking for."

"What did they do with it?"

"It's been a long time, been told down the line and confused, if they ever knew at all. One way it's come down is that the sphere was smashed to fragments the size of sand and buried at the church. Another has it that they shipped it off to Rome, and it's locked in the Vatican somewhere to this day. Another claims that the sphere never existed in the physical form, that it was just a metaphor for the ideas, philosophies, and predictions of Clastier. He called them Attestations and Divinations." She looked at Rip's bewildered face. "Poor boy, I have something that will clear up all this serious talk." Teresa left the room and Rip wondered if she might bring an Eysen back. Returning, her smile increased his excitement.

"Look at these," she said, pulling an arm from behind her back. "Shortbread cookies. I made them myself."

"Oh, they look delicious."

"Wait until you taste them."

He took one. "Amazing," he said around bites.

"This old half-baked broad can bake, huh?" she said, winking.

Rip laughed before turning serious again. "Teresa, what do you think happened to Clastier's sphere?"

"I think they smashed it."

He had a sudden feeling of being kicked in the stomach. "Why?"

"They couldn't risk its power getting into the hands of the common man."

"Clastier considered himself a common man; he used those words."

"I know. His story survived."

"Funny, they could destroy an object, but they couldn't quite extinguish the spirit of a man."

"It is part of an old story. His secret is part of an unspoken promise. Clastier says in one of those letters that 'A true secret is something angry at wanting to be released, but its only power comes from being kept.' He left clues to his secrets, didn't he? You must have found some to come all this way and ask an old woman about a forbidden name."

"Yes. I just wonder if it's enough."

"Then perhaps you haven't looked hard enough."

"There's something more?"

"The Clastier tales they told me growing up talked of papers that were hidden."

"I found those."

"Maybe you haven't found them all. Clastier had many friends and he knew his time was short, but most of all he was aware that the Church was the most powerful force in the world and precautions were needed. He knew what they would do. Things had to be preserved." She reached into the pocket of her housecoat and pulled out a stone fragment the size of Rip's hand. "It's part of the stone bowl that his sphere was found in," she said, passing him the piece.

Rip felt a lump form in his throat as he took it. Studying the carved stone for a moment, recalling the one he left in North Carolina, he knew they were identical. There were the familiar circles and beautifully carved lines. He was about to pull out his laptop and verify it against photos when the phone rang. Rip, so immersed in the fragment, hardly noticed Teresa walking back to the desk to answer, until she handed him the phone and said, "Mr. Ripley, it's for you."

twenty-four

Nanski and Leary left Taos on Highway 68 along the Rio Grand River, then through Española; it was the quickest route to Chimayó. Leary noticed Nanski's pensive mood as they drove. "What did the Cardinal say that has you so worried?"

"Clastier used to preach at Chimayó, but his true church was somewhere else. A wealthy and influential man, named Abeyta, built Chimayó as a private chapel in 1810. The building we'll see today replaced a smaller, earlier version in 1816. Clastier actually became a priest at a nearby church sometime in the 1830s; the location is secret to this day as it was leveled during the expunging of Clastier. The Cardinal has been unable to find any references to where the original Clastier site might be."

"If it was leveled, why does it matter?"

"Everything about Clastier matters!"

"Why?"

"Because just like with Malachy's hidden prophecies, Clastier also predicted that stone bowls contained the destruction of the Church."

"It's starting to feel like we're in the end times, like we're two warriors of God ordained to save Catholicism, the one true religion, and humanity's only hope for salvation."

Nanski didn't respond; Leary might sound dramatic, but he knew Leary believed his words. He stared at the Rio Grande River; working its way through the narrow canyon with just enough space for the river and the road, and decided Leary wasn't too far off. "Salvation or survival. We've got to stop him."

"You really think he'll be at Chimayó?"

"Gaines has whatever was contained in the bowls and he is going to every church where Clastier is known to have preached."

"What if Gaines knows the location of Clastier's original church?"

"That's a terrifying thought. We need to find him first."

"What else do we know about him?"

"In 1839, the bishop in Durango heard reports of Clastier's radical preachings and during 1840, they stripped him of his parish."

"Man, losing his church. What did Clastier do?"

"Sometime in the next year or so, he managed to win the confidence of Abeyta, who invited him to preach at Chimayó. It took until 1843 or '44 before he was officially defrocked."

"But he didn't quit his blasphemy, did he?"

"No. And Church leaders in Rome ordered him executed."

"Good move, he was a wicked man. But he got away?"

"It's unclear. Clastier went into hiding; first, at an unknown location near Chimayó; then, for a short time at the San Francisco de Asís Mission, where he had a sympathetic friend behind the pulpit. Finally, he fled to the

Taos Pueblo where the Indians hid him until he was
flushed out by a posse. From there, the story becomes
rumors and legends."

Kruse and Harmer were heading to Chimayó at the same
time. Booker's superior intel had given his AX agents a
slight head start, but Kruse chose to take the more scenic
High Road, figuring fugitives would always take the
backroads. He hoped to get lucky and find them before
they reached the historic church.

The FBI was also converging on Chimayó. In the
helicopter, Hall finished reading the manuscript of Gaines'
upcoming book, "The Future of the Past." With Gaines in
the news, wanted for murder, and then not; the publisher
was rushing the book to an earlier release, along with a
companion volume of deleted sections and excerpts from
Gaines' most controversial speeches.

The publisher had suddenly become the target of a
hostile takeover from a corporation that DIRT believed was
ultimately controlled by Booker. At the same time, several
religious groups had mobilized to pressure the company
not to release his work. The tactics just made them more
anxious to publish sooner – controversy is the best thing
for book sales.

Hall watched the ruggedly beautiful wilderness of
northern New Mexico flow beneath the chopper. He didn't
believe Gaines was a criminal, but surmised that the
famous archaeologist had found something that could
severely damage the reputation of the Church. However,
the reasons that Gaines seemed to want to protect the
Church eluded him. Booker's role was even less clear.
DIRT had uncovered many good deeds done in secret by

the ruthless tycoon, but with so many dead-ends and a long string of lawsuits and investigations swirling around Booker, a true picture couldn't be seen. Hall suspected even Barbeau might be coming around to a similar theory about Gaines; he planned to discuss it with him, after they landed at Chimayó.

The Sangre de Cristo Mountains seemed to explode out of the earth below and the irony of their name translated to "Blood of Christ" momentarily disturbed Hall. "What if Gaines really did find proof of Cosega? What if, as he said, 'the history of human origins on Earth is all wrong?' What if, in all the gaps that existed across millions of years of the Earth's history, another society actually existed?" he thought to himself, replaying the line that most haunted him: "The question is no longer what if it's wrong; the question is, how wrong is it?"

Gaines had spent his life searching for something impossible, and in that quest, he appeared to have made a discovery that shocked even him. He'd come to Virginia at the peak of his career; living a life anyone would envy. He left twenty-four hours later, with a price on his head, and little chance of escape. Whatever he found had to be extraordinary; the most powerful people in the world all wanted it. Hall suddenly realized that he might be the best chance Gaines had at survival, and the thought terrified him.

twenty-five

Rip looked at Teresa and then tentatively at the phone. "Hello."

He didn't recognize the voice at first, just a man yelling, "Get out, Gaines, you have to get out of there."

"Who is this?"

"It's Aragón, the historian. The FBI just left here. I tried not to tell them anything, but one of the kids had already mentioned overhearing me tell you about Chimayo."

"Damn it. Okay, thanks for calling."

"I'm sorry."

After he hung up, Teresa said, "Time's up, huh?"

"Yeah. A lot of people are still trying to silence Clastier, and destroy the sphere."

"You have to go to the church."

"No. There's no time."

"Remember time is different in New Mexico."

"People are after us."

"The church will only take a minute."

"I don't understand why they didn't destroy the church?"

"Because they located his sphere. They would have destroyed everything Clastier touched until they found it.

Oh, they still tore that chapel apart. My grandmother said it was taken down "to the innards" as they searched for any trace of the man who would become 'never to have been' but, there is one thing they could not remove."

"What?"

"The very thing that has made the El Santuario de Chimayó famous around the world."

Her dramatic pauses made him impatient. "Please, Teresa, I have no time."

"The dirt, poor boy, they couldn't remove the dirt."

"Dirt?"

"Your hand must touch the dirt; you must take some of it with you. I have given you the letters; do this for me." She smiled at his exasperated look. "They cannot hurt you there. You'll still manage your escape."

"Then I'm off." Rip hugged the old woman. "I could never thank you enough. You've taken what I already had, but couldn't accept, and returned it to me in a way that now it all makes sense."

She smiled. "And cookies, I also gave you the best damned cookies you've ever had." She handed him a brown bag. "Don't worry, it's only cookies. Oh, and a plastic baggy, you'll need it for the dirt."

He took the bag, along with the manila envelope, and hurried to the door, "Stay safe, great-, great-, *great*-granddaughter of Flora."

"And Clastier."

"Seriously?"

She laughed at Rip's shocked expression. "Apparently he never knew Flora was pregnant. But so much of the story is lost, maybe he knew, maybe he even saw the baby."

He hugged her again. "Incredible. There really is nothing new in the past."

Rip got in the backseat. "FBI's on the way. We gotta go."

"Which way?" Sean asked.

"A quick stop at the church and then to Española."

"The church, huh?" Gale laughed. "What on earth did that old lady have to say that could send you to another church?"

"Let's just say you would have liked her," Rip said.

"Do we really have time for sightseeing at some old church, if the FBI is on the way?" Sean asked. "What's so important?"

"It's a long story," Rip said.

"No problem, I've got nothing but time," Sean said.

"Let me run in here, first," Rip pointed to the church, as Sean circled close to the entrance. "You guys wait here. I won't be a minute."

"Are you kidding?" Gale said, miffed. "Did the old lady say we weren't allowed in here either?"

"Please," Rip shot her a pleading look. "I need to do this one alone." He jumped out and jogged toward the entrance.

Gale, already annoyed at being excluded from the conversation with Teresa, now felt even more removed from their quest. She started after him, but stopped a few feet from the car. Something had happened to Rip in that house. By insisting on going alone into the church, he seemed to be finally accepting Clastier's continued guidance. She decided not to interfere, but would demand the full story before the end of the day.

Two weathered pine doors clung to hinges and stood

permanently open under an adobe arch that led to the courtyard. A powerful wave of *déjà vu* mixed with dread made Rip dizzy for a few moments. He wove his way past several tourists and around a wooden cross at the center of the stone walkway. As he stepped inside, the two-hundred-year-old adobe church became timeless. Staring at a crucified Christ in the center of the colorful altar screens, Rip felt nauseous and unsteady. He looked around for something to support him and grasped the back of a wooden pew; the air was suffocating. He made his way down the center aisle of the nave, using the pews as crutches, until he reached the sanctuary. He fell through a small opening to his left and landed on his knees, staring into a shallow hole carved in the floor. He felt sure this wasn't his first visit there, as some strength returned. "Conway," Rip said, suddenly hoarse, remembering what the Pueblo shopkeeper had called him.

He pulled the baggy from his pocket and scooped the soft sacred dirt into it, then quickly placed it into his pack. The small room had its own exit. On the way out, a wall of crutches, crucifixes, walkers, and images of Christ; seemed to advertise proof of miraculous cures. The dirt attracted hundreds of thousands of seekers each year, many desperate to be healed or saved. He wasn't sure if it was his imagination, but Rip felt stronger.

He ran back to the waiting car. "Let's get out of here," he said, breathlessly.

"Do you hear that?" Sean asked.

The three of them concentrated on the quiet and heard the distant hum of an approaching helicopter. "Go!" Rip yelled.

twenty-six

Barbeau looked around, stared up at the three crosses on top of the simple adobe church, and shook his head. "This guy has Vatican agents chasing him; why the hell does he keep going to churches?" he asked himself.

The helicopter had landed in a nearby parking lot. Field agents would arrive soon in vehicles. Hall was already interviewing people, showing photos, taking names. That dreadful and familiar feeling of just having missed Gaines crept in leaving him unsure of everything. He looked around the odd collection of adobe buildings, his gaze resting on a stone archway that seemed out of place. It seemed like a metaphor of the entire investigation – nothing quite fit. There would be a more thorough search, as soon as backup arrived, but he could feel it – Gaines was gone again.

Barbeau wandered into the chapel. There were only seven "rooms" in the old building. Hall had already searched them all. The adobe walls were three feet thick. He appreciated the simplicity of these old churches; they all looked like they belonged right where they were, as if they'd always been there, formed of dirt, sun, and rain. Inside the sacristy, the hole in the floor seemed dug by a child; yet he knew what it was from a file prepared by a subordinate at Quantico. At least Barbeau knew what it was supposed to be. He squatted and dipped his hand into the powdery earth, let the grains run through his fingers, and caught himself saying a prayer. It wasn't for the capture of Gaines, or the exposure of the Attorney General's corruption. Special Agent Dixon Barbeau sat on the floor of this dusty little chapel in the middle of the high desert of New Mexico and silently prayed for his wife and daughter's forgiveness. A moment later Hall called his name from the sanctuary. Barbeau dropped about a thimbleful of dirt into a small evidence bag and shoved it into his pocket. "In here," he yelled, standing up.

"We've got a positive ID. Someone saw him here less than fifteen minutes ago."

"Did they see what he was driving?"

"Blue sedan, North Carolina plates."

"North Carolina? Interesting. Do we have a number?"

"Negative, but how many blue sedans with North Carolina plates could be within a fifteen-minute radius?"

"One is all we need; give it to state and local."

"Already done."

"Good man. Today just might be our day. Where's our crew?"

"ETA eight minutes."

"Okay, you wrap up here, leave two agents to work the vicinity, and get on the road with the others. I'm going back up in the air to see what I can see. I'll pick you up somewhere; hopefully at an arrest."

"Roger that."

Barbeau was gone when Nanski and Leary showed up. A field agent spotted them and alerted Hall. He couldn't resist the chance.

He snuck over to where they were parked. "Excuse me," he said, appearing at the driver's side window. "Either one of you know where I could find Ripley Gaines?"

"You might want to check with the FBI; I think they're in charge of that investigation," Leary said, coolly.

"That's good to hear you say that, Mr. Leary, because it sure seems like some people think the Vatican is running this."

"No sir, if the Vatican were leading the case, it would have been resolved in Virginia."

"If the Vatican weren't interfering, we might have settled things in West Memphis is what you probably meant to say."

"Can we help you, Agent Hall?" Nanski leaned over and asked.

"You bet your ass you can help me, Nanski. How about you two let the Bureau do their job and stop interfering with a federal investigation."

"Interfering? No sir," Leary said. "We're just a couple of private citizens out to see our beautiful country."

"Really? Do you think you're funny? Because I don't. I ought to arrest you right now. I might do that. How'd you like to spend the next few days in federal lockup?"

"We'd be out in ten minutes." Leary glared at him.

"Relax," Nanski said to Leary. "We don't want any trouble, Agent Hall. I'm sure you don't either."

"You clowns think you're a couple of righteous Christians? Well, where I grew up, Christians act a little differently, and chumps like you were just considered thugs."

"Were you gonna charge us with a crime?" Leary asked. "Or are you just wanting to preach a sermon?"

"No. I'm not going to arrest you today. But I promise I'll find something soon. And until then, stay the hell out of my way!"

Nanski got out of the car. "We'll do our best."

"Where are you going?" Hall asked.

"Just having a look around," Nanski replied.

"There's nothing to see. Gaines is long gone."

"No doubt. But we'd still like to check the place. I'm sure the Bureau is doing a fine job, and has everything under control; I just like to see for myself. I'm funny that way," Leary said, getting out.

"Leary, is that a cross carved in your hair?" Hall asked.

"I'll be happy to cut one into your hair. You want to look like me, Hall? Do you want to come to Jesus?" Leary turned back and reached inside the car.

Hall pulled his gun. "Hands where I can see them, Leary!"

Leary turned around, hands in the air, holding only a Bible. "Relax, Hall. I was just getting you a copy of the Holy Scripture. Jesus has a message for you."

"No thanks," Hall said, holstering his weapon.

"If you're all done with us, Agent Hall, we're going to head inside."

"I'll say a prayer for you," Leary sneered. "When was your last confession?"

Hall spoke into his radio, as the Vatican agents headed toward the church. A minute later they were intercepted by two suits. At first Leary resisted, but Nanski cautioned him. The FBI agents handcuffed the two men and led them to the back of a Bureau car. Hall waved at Leary as he departed the scene with a couple of other agents, hoping to catch up with Barbeau.

The feds left Nanksi and Leary in the car for a couple of hours, asked them a few questions, and then released them. Nanski called Pisano, who in turned called the Attorney General, who promised, "Heads will roll." Leary was furious, but drove carefully, because a state trooper had tailed them since they left the Church.

twenty-seven

Rip refused to talk, except to tell them he wanted to find a place to buy camping gear. He sat in the back, eating the rest of Teresa's cookies. Gale and Sean weren't interested in baked goods from "the crazy lady." The helicopter flew over twice and soon they were in Española; a place of traffic and fast food confusion. Sean, by far the least recognizable, was elected to go into the outdoor shop for the gear. Rip handed him five hundred dollars of Grinley's money and a list.

Once they were alone, Gale joined him in the back. "So are you going to tell me what you and Teresa talked about? And what was so important in the church that we practically had to wait around for the FBI to show up?" Gale asked.

"It's extraordinary. I don't know where to begin."

"Sean's probably going to be in there a while. Want to go for a quick walk along our river?" she asked.

"Our river?"

"The Rio Grande is right over there. The same river we rafted, so it's ours. Once you raft a river, you own it."

The NSA technician kept recording as Gale and Rip left the car. The listening devices could hear up to forty feet away, depending on background noises, most of which could be removed later if necessary. The tech was just doing his job and didn't much care one way or another, but Busman and his bosses were frustrated. They had two chase vehicles and a chopper just out of earshot. They weren't worried about them escaping, but they wanted to know everything Gaines knew; they needed every word recorded. Three more units were en route. Although patient, Busman knew the longer it took, the more likelihood that something could go wrong, and he wanted it over.

The way Busman saw it; the information Rip was sharing with Gale, as part of the sphere's puzzle, belonged to the NSA. The organization had extensive experience in accumulating minute threads of data over long periods of time, often under foreign or hostile conditions. This was no different, except the stakes were much higher than anything in which the NSA had ever been involved. Busman had a Kindle filled with books on military history and strategy. He'd been up late the night before finishing a work about the genius of Attila the Hun, and he knew victory had many definitions, as long as you won.

"The strangest thing," Rip began, as he and Gale stood on a low bluff over the Rio Grande, and unbeknownst to them, just out of range of the NSA mics. "Even as I walked into the courtyard at Chimayó, I felt as if I'd been there before."

"*Déjà vu?*"

"Much stronger than that. I'd never been there, but the feeling was overpowering, and then when I went inside the church, it felt as if I'd travelled back in time and was entering it two hundred years earlier."

"Like a past-life regression," she said, seriously.

"Gale, I don't believe in that stuff."

"But it happened."

"I'm a scientist. I've dug up enough of the past to know that the past doesn't go anywhere. When people die, they stop existing. I know it's no fun to think that when it's over, it's over; but we get one chance and then we become a relic."

"One chance at what?"

"To get it right."

"How do we know if we got it right? Why would we care? Do you really think we're all here to just get as rich and comfortable as we can? All this . . . " She swept her arm out to the Rio Grande, in the distance- its confluence with the Rio Chama, vast mesas and desolate mountains beyond. "All this is here for our one chance? Seems like an awful lot of trouble for visits to Walmart, reality TV shows, and weapons of mass destruction."

"Your 'airy-fairy' world is a dream. I deal in facts."

"Do you? What was that feeling in the church today? What about the shopkeeper recognizing you?"

"He didn't recognize me. He thought I was some guy named Conway."

"Conway who came for Clastier! Do you really need more proof?"

"Proof of what?"

"That you have lived before. That you're caught up in a karmic web of immense proportions and consequence."

"As if I have the whole universe in my hands."

"As if you do," she said staring. "You do," she whispered.

"I don't want to debate esoteric philosophy with you."

"What do you want?"

"I want to get some place where I can study the Eysen and talk about Clastier. You were right about the deep connections between them."

"What changed your mind?"

"Clastier's letters."

Her eyes widened.

"He wrote letters to Teresa's great-, great-, great-grandmother. He found another Eysen."

"Jee. Sus. Christ."

"Yeah."

"Where is it?"

"Vatican. Or they destroyed it. Hard to know."

"So he may not have been telling you to look for the one you found in Virginia? His papers may have been talking about the one he found."

"Yes."

"And that means there may be more Eysens," Gale said. "What if the Vatican has been collecting them? What if they've been part of our history all along? Where did they come from?"

"We have to find out, before they find us."

"Maybe they won't."

"No, Gale. The raid at Grinley's house tells us . . . they can find us, anywhere, and they will. It's only a matter of time."

Sean returned and as they drove west, Gale wrote in her journal. "I'm convinced Rip is close to recognizing who Conway really was. His admission that I've been right about the deep connections between Clastier and the Eysen is huge! But the biggest news of the day – we don't have the first Eysen. That means the world could have changed before, but it was intentionally stopped. What if that turns out to have been the right thing? What if there is something about the Eysen that is horrible?"

twenty-eight

Harmer and Kruse had watched with amusement, as Hall harassed and arrested the "Vatican boys." They'd pulled up just as it unfolded and stayed parked behind a low-rider with a dazzling paint job. Kruse decided not even to get out of the car. Instead they followed Hall and phoned Booker.

"I don't know what's going on," Booker said in a clipped tone. "I was hoping you would have good news."

"Well, at least Gaines is still eluding the competitors."

"Stay with the Bureau, guys. I'll call when I hear something."

The helicopter landed in the parking lot of an abandoned hardware store. Barbeau spoke with the Director while he waited for Hall to arrive.

"Yes, sir, we just got a lead that a state trooper has spotted the car near Santa Fe. They confirmed it was the same North Carolina plate. We got a match from a traffic camera in Ranchos de Taos, where someone picked up Gaines and Asher this morning. Odd thing though, the plate doesn't come up in NC's DMV. The resolution on the camera isn't great and a tech could have made a mistake, but it's strange and I don't like strange. More importantly, we couldn't make out who was driving."

"Attorney General Dover is meeting with the President as we speak. He's not happy about how the investigation's going. Actually accused me of not being forthcoming with facts and leads."

"What are they meeting about? Firing you again?"

"I'll find out soon. I'm meeting the two of them in an hour. And somehow I don't think they're finished with me yet. If they wanted me out, they wouldn't do it at Camp David," the Director said.

"I can't wait to hear."

"What's going on with the car now?"

"Hall will be here in about three minutes, and then we'll fly to the arrest. Troopers are tailing the car now. We might finally have him."

"Let me know, I'd love to have that information before I meet with the President."

Barbeau, anxious to get to the blue sedan and finally look Gaines in the eye, called Hall.

"Where the hell are you?"

"Two red lights away. I can see the chopper. I'll be there in a minute but, something you should know, I detained Nanski and Leary."

"Wish you hadn't done that. What'd you charge them with?"

"Nothing. Just holding them for questioning."

"The Director has a meeting with Dover and the President in an hour. Make sure they're cut loose by then."

"Will do, just wanted to make sure they didn't trip us up when we're so close. Hey, I'm pulling in now."

"Let's go finish this."

As Hall was running to the chopper, Barbeau confirmed the state police still had the car.

"We're two cars back, in a plain wrapper. We have three other units shadowing on a nearby route and our bird is ready," the officer in charge told him. Barbeau was smiling as they rose off the pavement and headed toward Santa Fe. He held up his hands to Hall, indicating ten minutes.

Hall nodded and thought, "Then what? We capture Gaines, then we need to keep the investigation going to the Attorney General's office, the Vatican, the President?" Arresting Gaines was only the beginning of something so big, Hall could not imagine not being consumed by it. He'd always known how big cases could destroy a marriage, so he avoided them. But he had a beautiful girlfriend he hadn't seen in too long. And there was something about this case, something so dark that at times, only the faintest light could shine through, and the light wasn't from where it should have been; everything was upside down. The Justice Department and the Church usually representing "right" were shrouded in darkness, and the only light came from the two fugitives. Hall's head pounded with the spinning rotors of the helicopter. He'd never had a premonition before, didn't even know if he believed in them, but something was telling him he wasn't going to live to see the resolution of this crushing case.

Barbeau pointed down, smiling. Hall saw the blue car. Barbeau gave an order in his headset, and the state police moved in and pulled the car over without incident. The pilot put them down in the blocked roadway fifty feet in front of the car. Barbeau and Hall jumped out. Barbeau yelled, "We got 'em!"

As they got closer, Hall saw two men and a woman being handcuffed, and his heart sank. "It's not them!"

"What?" Barbeau said, cupping his ear.

"That's not Gaines and Asher!"

Barbeau stopped fifteen feet from the car. He could see what Hall saw. They were roughly the same build and description, but they were not his targets. He ran to the one who looked most like Gaines and yanked him around by the shoulder. "Who the hell are you?"

Before the startled man could answer, Barbeau stepped around to check the license plate. It matched the one the traffic camera had shown Gale and Rip getting into that morning. "Who are you?" Barbeau repeated. "How did you get this car?"

The trooper handed Barbeau the man's ID. "Sir, he's from Baltimore. Byron Creighton. Business card says he's a stockbroker."

Barbeau shook his head. "And the woman?"

"His wife, Pam."

"What are you doing in New Mexico, Creighton?"

"On vacation."

"If you're from Maryland, why are you driving with North Carolina plates?"

"It's a rental. Look, if I was speeding, this is a little over the top."

"Shut up. Haven't you been Mirandized?"

"Meringue-what?" Creighton answered.

"Don't get smart, you low-life."

"Easy," Hall said to Barbeau "He's on vacation."

"He is *not* on vacation," Barbeau shouted. "Does the car check out? Is it a rental?"

"We're still waiting word," the trooper said.

Hall pulled Barbeau away from the car. "What's going on? We got the wrong car. Let's get back up in the air and find the right one."

"Come on, Hall, you're a better agent than this. We got the wrong car on purpose. They switched and sent us on this wild-goose chase so Gaines could get away. The plate matches the traffic camera. You saw the stills of Gaines getting into this car hours ago."

"You think Gaines is so sophisticated that he had look-a-likes and another vehicle on standby?"

"No, but the NSA is."

"They're trying to capture him, not help him get away."

"Apparently not."

"Why would they help him escape? Booker maybe, but not the NSA."

"It's the NSA."

"Why are you so sure? Because Creighton is too cool? He knows we can't touch him, and Booker's people would have just pulled Gaines and Asher out. They'd be in Mexico by now."

"Why wouldn't the NSA just pull him?"

"I don't know. They need him out. Maybe he has some– wait, I've got it. What does Gaines do? He finds stuff. There is still something to find and they need him to do it."

The trooper came over and interrupted. "The plate is bogus. The car is registered to the U.S. Government."

"Let me guess," Barbeau said. "Division is classified."

"Correct," the surprised trooper answered.

Barbeau walked into the sagebrush, while he waited for the Director to get on the line. Hall followed. "I want to find out what he wants us to do now. How are we supposed to capture fugitives if they're being aided by the NSA?" Barbeau said, squinting back at the three "actors" handcuffed by the car. "And what do we do with those imposters?"

The Director's voice mail came on. Barbeau hung up. "Damn it, he must already be with the President. Charge those three with obstruction of justice. They're not to get phone calls until I speak with the Director."

Hall conveyed the orders to the trooper and exchanged contact information. As the helicopter lifted off again, Hall realized they were all out of leads, and wondered where they were going. He asked Barbeau through the headsets.

"We're going to the place where secrets hide."

twenty-nine

Rip was bothered by Gale's talk of reincarnation. He hadn't admitted to her that he felt a similar but milder form of *déjà vu* at the Pueblo Church ruins, and again at the San Francisco de Asís Mission Church. Taos Mountain, the whole Sangre de Cristo range, in fact, and the gorge all seemed strangely familiar.

He'd read only a fraction of Clastier's letters, but was intrigued by twice seeing Clastier's notes to Padre Garcia, whose church was located between Taos and Las Trampas. He could tell by Clastier's words to Flora that he and Garcia were close. Perhaps those letters had also survived. The archaeologist in him wanted to tell Sean to turn around and head back to Las Trampas, but that would be back into the hornet's nest they had only narrowly escaped. He needed to get into the Eysen, his Eysen. He still couldn't believe there was another. Everything was different now that he understood Clastier wasn't merely prophesying, but had actually looked into the magic ball and seen what Rip had.

They were now loaded with camping gear and food, and would hopefully soon be lost on the back roads heading into the wilds of northern Arizona. Rip watched the wickedly beautiful, inhospitable landscape pass and wondered what it would have been like in Clastier's time. Not much had changed except the ability to travel on paved roads in automobiles. Clastier had fled Vatican agents under primitive conditions but he didn't have to contend with instant communication, satellite tracking, and modern weaponry. Rip checked his pack, the gun, cash, and flashlight Grinley had so kindly given to him. He was a stranger on the run, a man in trouble.

Poor Grinley owed him nothing, and had become another victim in this grueling race. Rip tallied the cost again, as he had taken to doing in the quiet times – Josh Stadler, Larsen Fretwell, Ian Sweedler, Topper. Was Fischer dead? How else had they found Grinley? That meant they had likely found and killed Fischer and Tuke. The cops and Booker had also lost people. How many more would die?

Thinking about Booker's involvement brought back the betrayal in West Memphis. He didn't want to believe Booker would turn him in to the authorities. He'd known about Booker's more public, ruthless side, but over the years he'd also witnessed Booker's obsession with archaeology. They'd talked at length about Rip's Cosega theory. Other than Larsen and Rip, no one knew or cared more about Cosega. Booker actually seemed more fixated than Rip. He was especially fascinated with Clastier. Although Rip had never shown him the papers, Booker sometimes talked as if he'd read them.

Now Rip felt responsible for keeping Sean and Gale safe, and hoped it never came down to a choice between saving them or the Eysen.

"Damn it!" Sean said suddenly. "A road block."

They had just come around a bend. There was no way to turn around. Rip's hand clutched the door handle.

"What do I do? What do I do?" Sean yelled.

A police officer stood in the middle of the road, halting traffic with his arm. Rip looked back and saw several cars behind them, guardrails on either side. They couldn't even get out of the car without being seen.

"Keep going. Slow down and then just zoom past," Gale said, her pulse quickening. "You can get around that tow truck."

A pickup truck was on the shoulder ahead, its door open. Beyond it and behind the cop, a giant tow truck had lines extending over the ravine beyond their line of vision. A sheriff's car, a state police vehicle, and another wrecker also cluttered the road ahead. They were trapped.

"It'll take them two minutes to have us all in cuffs!" Gale shouted.

"Even if we could get around, that would just attract attention. They'd be all over us," Rip said. "But this isn't for us; there's been an accident. They're pretty busy, maybe they won't recognize us."

"What do I do?" Sean asked again.

"Stay calm."

The trooper yelled but they couldn't understand him.

"Someone's coming!" Gale said as another man dressed in jeans and a t-shirt approached the car.

"It's a pretty bad wreck," the man said from a few feet away. "Car went over the embankment. The driver was messed up something terrible; he might not make it. They already got him to the hospital."

Sean couldn't respond.

"I saw the whole thing, called it in on my cell phone. Wanna see pictures?" He started working his phone, walking toward the car.

Sean waved him off.

"Oh, yeah, pretty grizzly stuff," he looked disappointed not to be able to share his eyewitness coverage. The line of cars was growing longer behind them. The second tow truck moved out of their lane. "Look up and smile, you're on TV," the man said to them. The sound of a helicopter surged Rip's adrenaline.

Gale leaned into the windshield, looked up and saw it. "News helicopter," she said, only a little relieved.

Suddenly, the trooper signaled them to proceed.

"Bueno-bye," the man with the cell phone said, waving as they passed.

Sean pulled ahead slowly, none of the cops even glanced at them. A minute later, they were back up to fifty miles per hour and clear.

Sean checked the rearview mirror and recognized Busman's vehicle behind them. No one had noticed an NSA operative sliding around the car and quietly placing magnetic New Mexico license plates over the North Carolina ones while the man talked to them about the accident. That man was also a highly trained agent; he hadn't really seen the accident, because there hadn't been one. Even the news chopper was bogus. It was all a staged distraction, so the NSA could continue to insure the FBI would not find Gaines. Often things aren't what they appear, Sean thought.

thirty

Kruse and Harmer were tailing the FBI agents back to Taos, when Booker reached them. "Forget the FBI," he said. "They have no idea what's happening. Chart a new course. You're going to Arizona."

"According to the dossier you sent, Rip's father lives in Flagstaff. But he wouldn't be that dumb, would he?" Kruse asked.

"Rip is anything but dumb. He knows the feds know where his father lives, but Rip has spent a lot of time in Arizona and knows it fairly well, so anything is possible. I think the feds and the Vatican have lost the trail, and will likely figure Flagstaff is a probable destination for Rip; so we need to make sure we get him before he gets there."

"Any clues as to which route?"

"Yeah. Back roads. My guess is 550 to 64."

"Cool, we'll pick it up in Española." Kruse said, pulling into a gas station to make a U-turn.

"One more thing. The NSA is tracking his car, so we have to deal with their involvement."

"Why haven't they just grabbed him?"

"Because they know what he has and need his cooperation. But Gaines also knows what he has and would never knowingly give them his cooperation.

"We're going to need some help."

"I'm working on it."

Barbeau and Hall checked into a motel. Other agents would arrive soon. In the meantime, they walked to a nearby restaurant recommended by the desk clerk and ate a fine authentic New Mexican meal of burritos and burgers smothered in green chilies. The Director's personal assistant was calling, as they were finishing, and informed Barbeau that the Director would not be in touch until morning. Barbeau couldn't believe it. He wanted to know about the meeting with Dover and the President; but more than that, he needed to make him aware of the NSA's interference, and was desperately hoping for some input from the Director. "Maybe he's being held," Barbeau said, sarcastically.

"Hey, don't joke about that," Hall said. "The Attorney General, being corrupt with the President's knowledge, is a little too Watergate for me. This whole thing, Senator Monroe and Asher, Booker, the Vatican running around killing people;, it's testing the edge of my sanity. But the NSA, who might be able to hear our conversation right now; aiding in the escape of fugitives, being pursued by the FBI . . . that's beyond crazy. Doesn't it just scare the hell out of you?"

"Do you recall, back at the Academy during training, we were asked to create a scenario as bad as we could imagine? And then, the instructor would take us through it, step-by-step, as to how to break it down, investigate, resolve?"

"Yeah, Quantico was a long time ago, but that's one exercise that sticks out. We came up with some horrific stuff."

"We did, too, but nothing close to this. Am I scared? Hell yes, Hall. I'm terrified. The Vatican may see what Gaines found as something that could destroy the Catholic Church; but I'm more concerned that this case could destroy something far more fragile . . . the United States Constitution."

"Good. I thought it might just be me." He looked across the table, as Barbeau put down his soda. "Because, you know what this looks like? The only thing standing in the way of a silent *coup d'état* is the Director of the FBI."

"And us."

"Great. And us," Hall said. "And the Director just spent a couple of hours with the enemy and he's gone dark. It doesn't look good."

"Do you even know who the enemy is?"

"It's supposed to be Gaines and Asher; maybe Booker Lipton. Instead, it's more like the U.S. Attorney General, the National Security Agency, a U.S. Senator, and maybe the President of the United States."

"Don't forget the Pope."

"We're screwed."

"Kind of feels that way." Barbeau signed the credit card receipt and stood up. "But remember, we have one secret weapon that none of the others have."

"What's that?"

"We're right."

"How do you know?"

Barbeau shot him a confused look. "How do I know? Because I'm so rarely wrong, that it actually causes me physical pain, when it happens."

Hall laughed. "Well then, I guess I chose the right side."

Barbeau nodded seriously, then made some calls, as they walked back to the motel. In the morning, they would meet with the historian, visit Taos Pueblo where the tribal police had interviews set up with the tour guide, the shopkeeper and his thugs, and if all went well, the state police might locate Grinley. Taos had many secrets; Barbeau planned to uncover as many as he needed to find out why the Vatican and the NSA were so intent on getting the artifacts, and if he could figure that out, he might just be able to locate Gaines and bring him in safely. However, the morning would hold a different kind of surprise.

thirty-one

After a while, Gale took over the driving. They were heading west, into the sun, and the glare was giving Sean a headache. U.S.-550 is the kind of road that ribbons across the wide-open desert, and on a hot summer evening you can almost see a band of cowboys, lost in time, galloping across the sagebrush in a cloud of dust. Farmington was the last big town. After that, traffic, already thin, would trickle down to almost nothing. The NSA was staying well back as to not raise suspicions, and they had other ways of tracking. Busman wasn't worried.

Sean stayed quiet as Gale and Rip discussed plans. "We'll make it to Canyon de Chelly tonight and put all this great camping gear to use."

"Thanks for getting all that, Sean," Gale said.

"Sure, I like shopping when someone else pays," Sean said. "Why Canyon de Chelly?"

"I've got a buddy there who will hide us for as long as necessary," Rip said.

"Canyon de Chelly is on the Navajo Reservation, right? So your friend is Navajo?" Gale asked.

"Yeah, is that okay?"

"Of course. I'm just making sure three white fugitives will be welcome in Indian country," Gale said, laughing.

"The Navajo Nation is the largest Native American reservation. We're talking more than 27,000 square miles across northeastern Arizona, and stretching into New Mexico and Utah."

"Sounds like a great place to hide."

"It's very remote. And Tahoma is a good friend; we met eight or nine years ago on a dig."

"Can the government trace your friendship?" Gale asked.

"Not likely," Rip said. The NSA technician in charge of monitoring the audio in the car couldn't help but smirk.

"Thanks to Sean showing up, we may have finally lost the feds. Now maybe we'll have time to figure this thing out."

When they stopped for gas at a busy Farmington station, Sean went to the restroom. Busman came in after him and found Sean standing in front of a urinal.

"We need more conversation about the Eysen."

"Rip already suspects something. I don't want to be too pushy."

"We've heard no indication he suspects anything."

"You aren't looking at his face."

"Relax, Sean. Everything is going great," Busman smiled, but then turned serious. "Our patience isn't endless. I'd like to have all the details we need in the next twenty-four hours. Think you can handle that?"

"No."

"Yes, you can."

"I'm just not sure what to do."

"Be yourself. Right now, you're acting too nervous. Joke around with them. Flirt with Gale."

"I'm not really in a joking mood."

"This is important. Remember our deal. You get what you want, we get what we want."

"Okay, I'll try."

"Good. And Sean-don't forget to wash your hands."

A distant thunderstorm created an explosive sky of cumulonimbus clouds, lightning, and large patches of blue and dark purple, all while the sun set behind the otherworldly rock formation called Shiprock.

"What a sight," Gale said, looking up from her journal. "Do you feel the electricity in the air? Something amazing is happening."

"What?" Sean asked, trying to sound light. He was driving again, said it made the trip go faster for him. He kept his thoughts on simple things, rather than the tragedy his life had become over the last week.

"I wish I knew," Gale said. "But something is definitely happening. And I have a feeling we'll know soon."

For some reason, Gale's mystical tone made Sean even more nervous and caused him to, once again, withdraw. Busman's car was so far back now he could only see it on long open straight-aways, of which there were too many for his liking.

"Navajo call it *Tsé Bit'a'í*, meaning 'winged rock' the Anglo name is Shiprock," Rip began. "It's a twenty-seven-million-year-old volcanic formation, but interestingly, the Navajo creation story cites the sacred peak as bringing their people to this land."

"Maybe there's an Eysen hidden there?" Gale said.

"What do you mean?" Sean took advantage of the opening.

"Nothing," Rip said.

"He's earned the right to know," Gale said.

"I'm just trying to keep him alive," Rip said.

"Funny, I thought I was trying to keep you alive," Sean shot back.

"Look, Sean, I appreciate all you've done. Your parents have lost one son. I don't want to be responsible for another death," Rip said.

Sean gripped the wheel tighter and clenched his teeth.

"Everyone who has seen or even learned of the Eysen is dead," Rip finished as lightning punctuated his words.

"Not you and Gale," Sean said.

"Come on, Rip," Gale said, "He's been in this from the beginning. His brother was the first casualty. He's wanted and running just like us. Sean got us out of Virginia, and Taos."

Rip thought quietly for a few minutes. The sky lit an intense electric aqua color against apocalyptic clouds that fortunately were moving away from them to the south. The sunset was stunning in the dramatic sky and Rip was grateful they would avoid the storm.

Sean didn't want to push anymore; his headache was almost gone and he hoped to avoid another argument. With the sun finally below the horizon, driving became easier, but he could feel Busman's eyes burning into the back of his head, and he knew the NSA man could hear every word.

thirty-two

Rip exhaled. "We found a kind of computer – an eleven-million-year-old computer."

"What do you mean?" Sean, genuinely surprised, didn't understand how anything that old could even be compared to a computer. "Like a stone abacus or something?"

"No. We're talking about a fully functioning computer. Kind of like an iPad except it resembles a bowling ball."

"I never did too well in history, or earth sciences, or whatever this is, but I'm pretty good on a computer, and what you're saying sounds impossible. It doesn't make sense."

"Of course it doesn't make sense. That's why they're killing people for it. And since when did killing ever make sense?" Gale said, not looking up from her writing.

"Who's doing the killing?" Sean asked, angrily.

"The Vatican killed Josh," Rip said.

Suddenly Sean jerked the car to the shoulder and got out, leaving the door open. He ran into the middle of the asphalt, still hot from the day's battle with the sun. Fortunately, no cars were visible in the twilight other than a distant set of headlights long behind them that appeared to have stopped. Gale ran after him.

"I don't believe it!" Sean screamed, his hands on his head. "Why are you lying to me?"

"It's true, I'm sorry. It's a hard thing to hear," Gale said, trying to hug him.

He pushed her away. "My girlfriend is Catholic, the Pope is Catholic, John F. Kennedy was Catholic, and you want me to believe their church, *any* church, murdered my brother over a computer, over ANYTHING?"

"It doesn't matter if you believe it," Rip said, standing next to the car. "It's what happened. The Vatican wants the Eysen, and it's hardly the first time they've killed over it."

"I'm not talking about history; I'm talking about now!"

"You want to talk about now after they murdered your brother? They killed a lab technician, just because Josh had taken the casing that held the Eysen to him."

"You sent him to do that."

"And I regret that. But the Church is doing the killing, not me. They also killed a man who helped raise me, and probably others who were just trying to do the right thing."

"What are you talking about?" He charged at Rip, but stopped short. "How do you know? Last I heard you were wanted for killing the lab guy."

"I told you this was a bad idea," Rip said calmly to Gale. "Let me have the keys, Sean. I don't think you should be driving right now."

"We know who killed them," Gale said, "because we have people helping us who know."

"Who? Who could know that? Who would even believe it? Someone just told you the *Vatican* killed my brother, and you think that sounds reasonable? What if I told you it was a drug dealer that killed him . . . or maybe it was OJ Simpson. No, no, it was a one-armed man."

"May I please have the keys?" Rip tried again, looking in both directions. Still no cars.

"Let me see the computer," Sean said, looking past Rip, into the car.

"The Eysen doesn't work at night."

"Of course it doesn't!" Sean rolled his eyes.

"Sean, I know you're upset," Gale began. "But this is not the place. We're standing in the middle of the road. All we need is for a cop to cruise by and we're all finished. Let's get to the canyon and we'll show you everything in the morning. You may not believe who killed Josh, but don't judge until you hear the whole story."

He shook his head. Gale thought he looked suddenly younger. "Fine. But I'm driving," he slammed the door.

"Okay," Gale said, shooting Rip a look to silence his protests. For the next hour, to the annoyance of Busman, there was almost no talking. Gale found a penlight in the glove box, used the time to read the Clastier Papers, and write in her journal. She wanted to press Rip more about what Clastier's letters contained, but knew he'd never discuss it while Sean could hear. She'd find a time.

Rip was now desperate for time to figure out Clastier and the Eysen. He thought about the friend he was counting on to hide them; Tahoma had worked with Rip and Larsen on a rarely authorized dig near Shiprock. Several startling artifacts were unearthed; nothing like the Eysen, but nonetheless, things that may have been far older than conventional wisdom allowed – twenty thousand years or more. The sponsor wanted to go further, but the Navajo Nation Government demanded they stop, citing religious concerns. Legal issues complicated matters, and although the find could have helped prove the Cosega theory; Rip sided with the Navajo and got Booker involved. This ended the dig, and his relationship with the sponsor.

During the same negotiations with the Navajo, it had come to light that an eastern university had done a dig nearby in the 1930s, and had taken sacred artifacts. The Navajo sought their return, but were refused. Prior to what would have been a lengthy and expensive court battle that was not going to be easy to win, Rip once again quietly enlisted Booker's help; and, between the two of them, they were able to secure the return of all the items.

Rip had made many sacrifices to the detriment of his career. He knew it was the right thing to do, but now wondered if he'd been able to prove Cosega back then, would he have wound up in Virginia? Would Larsen be alive? Larsen had been instrumental in convincing Rip to side with the Navajo, and so had Tahoma's sister, Mai. She had worked as a local guide on the dig. Larsen and Mai became quick friends, but it had been Rip who loved her.

Rip was relieved finally to be at Canyon de Chelly. He felt safe among the Navajo and was eager to get back into the Eysen in the morning. He phoned Tahoma from a battered payphone in front of a convenience/souvenir store. Twenty minutes later, a thirty-year-old green and white pickup truck arrived.

In the flickering fluorescent light of the store's sign, Sean could see Gale; staring at him. "Are you okay?"

"Yeah. I'm just tired, really tired."

"You like camping?"

"Yeah, Josh and I used to go a lot."

"I've camped with Josh, too, on another continent. A couple of them actually."

Sean smiled. But it faded quickly. Busman was out there in the blackness. He wasn't sure where or how, but he had a feeling he'd seen him smile and didn't approve.

A tall, lean man climbed from the truck; his long, black hair pulled back through a dark bandana atop his head. He hugged Rip. "I'm glad you've come, brother," Tahoma said. Introductions were made to the others. "Forget camping, you can stay with me," he said.

"Really, Tahoma, a good place to camp is all we need."

He stared at Rip. "Trouble follows you, my friend; it is in your eyes." The dirty fluorescents barely lit the area enough for Gale to see her own feet, and she wasn't sure how Tahoma could read their situation in Rip's eyes.

"That's a fact," Rip answered. "And I'm sorry to bring it close to your home."

"Your trouble is my trouble. You come to the house."

"No," Rip said, firmly.

"This trouble is serious," Tahoma said, looking from Rip to Gale and then to Sean, where his eyes lingered. "Okay." He turned back to Rip. "I'll take you to a good place, where the spirit of my people is strong."

They followed in their rental car over washboard roads and down steep rocky grades. The openness soon ceded to trees and the way became less passable. Suddenly, Tahoma stopped, leaving on the high beams. It would be on foot from there. They carried their gear to a flat area just beyond the headlights' range. Tahoma and Rip pitched a tent near an existing fire pit, while Gale and Sean put up another next to it. The idea was that Sean and Rip would share a tent, and Gale would have her own. But midway through the setup process, Gale changed the plan.

"I think I'd prefer to squeeze in with you guys," she said.

"Sure. I just thought you might want some privacy," Rip said.

"I think I gave up privacy ten days ago. How many beds have we shared since then?"

"Right. Okay," Rip said, unsure why he felt embarrassed.

Rip walked Tahoma back to his truck. "I truly am sorry to come here. I had nowhere else to go."

"This is where you should be, brother," Tahoma said.

"You haven't even asked about the trouble."

"We're not so far removed from civilization that I did not hear of an old friend being accused of murder."

"I've killed no one."

"You don't need to tell me that; even if I hadn't also heard they dropped the charges. But sadly, your face says there is more than that."

"Yes. People after us . . . powerful people."

"Tomorrow, I'll take you deep enough that you cannot be found. A place where my people have often sheltered from the wickedness of this world."

"I'd appreciate that," Rip nodded. "The same people were after Larsen . . . he's dead."

"I know. We saw it in the same report about you. I'm sorry. Larsen was a good man."

"One of the best."

"He's with the ancestors now; he'll reach into this world and right wrongs."

"If that's possible, then some people better be looking over their shoulders."

"Don't screw up your present moment by worrying about those other people. You're in Indian country now."

thirty three

Thursday July 20ᵗʰ

The historian told Barbeau and Hall about Clastier, without ever actually saying his name. Only after a long, and Barbeau thought absolutely ridiculous guessing game; was Hall able to spell it letter by letter. Barbeau had guessed Rumpelstiltskin and Rosebud as names, much to the historian's outrage.

"Clastier? You're afraid to say the name Clastier?"

"It is forbidden by the Pope," the historian proclaimed.

"Easy, Barbeau," Hall said. "This man was born a Catholic; have some respect."

"I didn't know you were born a Catholic. I thought you were indoctrinated," Barbeau said.

"I'd like you out of my house now," the historian said.

"Of course you would," Barbeau said, looking at a wall filled with carved wooden images of saints. "We can leave right away, but you'll be coming with us, in handcuffs, charged with aiding and abetting."

"I thought the murder charges had been dropped against Professor Gaines."

"True, but Gaines is wanted for things you have no idea about." Barbeau sat on the couch and put his feet on the coffee table. "If you knew how tired I am of this chase, how fed up I am with the Vatican's interference, or how serious this really is; I think you would be a little more cooperative."

The historian just frowned.

"Please forgive Agent Barbeau," Hall said. "Peoples' lives are at stake. You seem like a nice man. We need your help."

"I'll tell you what I know because I think it will hasten his departure," the historian said, glaring at Barbeau." And he did. He relayed, with almost perfect accuracy, every word exchanged between Gale, Rip, and himself. He omitted the phone call he made to Teresa's house, but worried that might be discovered later, if they checked his phone records. At this time, he thought it was the wisest course.

Barbeau and Hall would visit Teresa later, but next on the schedule was interviewing the key witnesses from Gale and Rip's escapades at the Pueblo. First, they stopped by their temporary office at the New Mexico State Police building.

"Ask the captain if they've made any progress on the drug dealer," Barbeau said to Hall, as they walked inside. Finding Grinley would be a huge break, since he'd spent considerable time with Gaines and Asher. But Hall was worried the Vatican may have already found and killed him.

Barbeau entered the conference room that had become their makeshift command center and was shocked to see the Director of the FBI. "This can't be good," Barbeau said. "If you flew all the way from Washington to Taos, New Mexico, did you even sleep last night?"

"Let's go for a walk," the Director said. "Leave your phone here."

They passed Hall, coming back from the captain's office. "Director, we didn't know," he looked at Barbeau. "We didn't know he was coming, did we?"

"No," Barbeau said. "Should Agent Hall join us?" Barbeau asked the Director.

"Sorry, Hall. I need Barbeau alone for a brief word. Nothing personal. We'll definitely get you up to speed later."

"Sure thing. I've got plenty to do," Hall said, trying not to sound annoyed.

Once they were outside, the Director continued walking far into the sagebrush that surrounded the building. Barbeau just missed stepping on a large prickly pear cactus, its dried blooms looking like forgotten pink confetti.

"What's so important that you couldn't tell me over the phone?" Barbeau asked, hoping he didn't sound as impatient as he felt.

"There is no way to trust the privacy of any telephone, even the scrambled ones, and certainly not one originating from the D.C. area."

"The NSA?"

"And others. The loss of our citizens' privacy happened long ago. What's more alarming is that no privacy remains, even for officials."

"Some would call that fair."

"Not when the information gleaned is used to manipulate and control. We're not talking about a utopian transparency, where all is done in the name of right and good. This is a long-organized conspiracy to usurp power from the people, and it's probably too late to stop it."

"But Director, isn't it our job to stop it?"

"Of course it is. Damn it, that's why I'm here. But I've got a family, who also depend on me."

Barbeau knew the Director had to know about his personal life. He might even know more about its current status than he himself did, so he assumed the jab was unintentional. "Have you been threatened, sir?"

"Hell, yes, I've been threatened." He stared off toward the Weimer foothills.

"Did the Attorney General threaten you?"

The Director did not speak.

Barbeau looked around, unconsciously hoping Hall would appear. He was much better at these delicate conversations. "Did the President of the United States threaten you?"

"It's not that simple. The President isn't corrupt, but he has been corrupted. The NSA has its tentacles everywhere. They don't really work for the President anymore; it's the other way around."

Barbeau understood; the Director's very presence in Taos meant it was true. "Can't the President just fire people, cut out the cancer?"

"They'd kill him."

"By that, you mean assassination?"

"I brought that up at the meeting and the Attorney General said, 'Assassinations are so old-fashioned. They're too obvious. There are a hundred ways to destroy a person and if death is the chosen avenue, then something far more creative than a madman with a gun can be arranged.' It's an Orwellian, Kafkaesque nightmare." He looked at Barbeau through bloodshot eyes. "But there may be a way."

"A way to what?"

"To stop the NSA, and the power elite who control them, to wrestle control back where it belongs, and to restore the balance of power."

Barbeau held the Director's glance. "Does this way include the possibility that we wind up dead by one of those 'creative means' the Attorney General alluded to?" Barbeau asked.

"Look, Dixon, we're damned if we do . . . the thing is, we either go compliant, and watch as our country becomes something our grandfathers would never recognize, or we fight."

"How do we fight something like this?"

"They have fear on their side. Even as a kid, I knew that if I was fighting someone whose strongest weapon was fear, I would eventually win. Fear may be scary in the dark, but get it into the light of day and fear turns out to be surprisingly weak."

"Are the President and Attorney General compliant or fighting?"

"That's why I flew two thousand miles."

thirty-four

Gale, Rip, and Sean were awake and munching on trail bars when Tahoma arrived with a surprisingly deluxe hot breakfast.

"Thank you," Rip said. "This is too much."

"Where did you get this?" Gale asked in amazement. She felt as if they were a million miles from the modern world.

"My sister made it," Tahoma answered, exchanging a glance with Rip. "She is a warrior in the kitchen."

"How is Mai?" Rip asked. Gale detected a soft and hopeful tone in Rip's voice.

"She's as much of a firecracker as you remember."

"It's been a while. I should have kept in touch," Rip said, while chewing on a flatbread sandwich of vegetables and eggs that might have been the tastiest thing he'd ever eaten.

"Probably you should have," Tahoma said. "But the seasons are different in dreams."

Gale thought it an odd statement, but Rip nodded as if it were profound logic; as if he'd heard it many times before. She was envious of how easily Tahoma wore his spirituality.

"Sean, I brought you a cola," Tahoma said, fishing a cold can from a small cooler.

"Thanks! My favorite breakfast beverage," Sean said, noticing that Gale and Rip got tea.

Tahoma nodded, his eyes squinting during a lingering stare. He smiled. "When y'all done eating, I'll take you deeper."

"Thanks, Tahoma . . . for everything."

Tahoma started breaking down the unused tent. Gale grabbed their stuff from the other one. "Your eyes tell a story," Tahoma said to her.

She'd heard similar pick-up lines countless times, but she suspected Tahoma meant it in a different way. "How do you see so much?"

He thought for several seconds. "It seems that in your society everything exists on two separate levels: there is the living and there's the dead. There are humans and animals, known and unknown, the latest news and the long forgotten. Everything is separate." He tossed their sleeping bags in the back of his truck. "My people have always understood that it is easier to walk between the worlds. Otherwise, you're half-blind."

Rip rode with Tahoma, while Sean and Gale followed in the rental. When the canyon finally came into view, it seemed like a vision, something that could hardly be real. Lacking the magnificence of the Grand Canyon or the drama of Bryce Canyon, Canyon de Chelly, instead, had a mystical sense to it – littered with ruins, petroglyphs, and sacred sites, while also being a living community of farms, ranches, and orchards.

"Incredible," Gale said to Tahoma once they parked the rental and she squeezed in front, between him and Rip. Sean rode in the open back of the truck.

"Hang on back there," Tahoma said to him through the sliding window, "It's gonna get a little bumpy."

"Have your people always lived here?" Gale asked.

"They say our ancestors, the Anasazi, have lived in the canyon for five thousand years," he said, then leaned over toward Rip, "but it has been much longer." Gale assumed Tahoma knew of Rip's Cosega theory. The colorful cliffs had been formed over millions of years. "It's actually three connecting canyons, with many hiding places," Tahoma added, laughing.

Two hours later, after they'd been on the canyon floor for a while, he stopped below an ancient cliff dwelling; that, at first, Gale didn't notice because it so perfectly matched the surrounding rock. Tahoma produced sandwiches that were beyond delicious. "Your sister?" Gale asked.

"Yeah, Mai doesn't like people to be hungry," Tahoma said. Another hour and a half of boulders, ruts, and dense vegetation robbed the truck of enough road to continue. "It's just a short hike now."

They made their way into a poet's glen. A large open cave met a canopy of cottonwood trees, completely obstructing the area from the rim, nearly a thousand feet above. A spring fed a stream and the meadows nearby were almost entirely shielded by outcroppings of rocks and trees.

"Wow, it's tailor-made as a hideout," Rip said, smiling.

"My people needed to hide many times," Tahoma said. He helped them set up their tents. "I've got to get going, but I'll be back in the morning. You're well stocked with provisions."

"Thank you again, Tahoma. Please give my best to Mai, and thank her, too."

"I will. She might ride along with me in the morning."

"I'd love to see her again," Rip said.

Sean went off to explore the area, which gave Gale and Rip another chance to debate whether to include him in their studies of the Eysen. "I don't know how you're going to avoid showing it to him," Gale said. "We're all stuck down here together. You can't just wander off to a sunny spot, spend hours watching it, and think he's just going to sit by the stream all day."

"Why not?"

"Because, Rip, we'd still be in Taos without him. We probably would have been arrested that first day up on the Blue Ridge Parkway."

"Why do you keep defending him?"

"He's my friend's little brother. My dead friend, who I helped kill."

"You?"

"Josh wouldn't have taken the casing to the lab, if I hadn't gone along with it."

"Were you two sleeping together?"

"What kind of question is that?"

"An inappropriate one. I'm sorry."

"We've been together almost every minute for the past ten days, and you still find new ways to annoy me. What if Josh and I were lovers, what if we were going to be married? How does that matter? He's dead." Gale walked off in tears.

Rip followed. "Gale, I didn't mean, I mean to say, I wasn't . . . "

"No, you weren't. That's the problem with brilliant people; they're always selfish. Why is that?"

"I wouldn't know. Haven't I just proven I'm anything but brilliant?"

"You've proven you're arrogant. That's all."

"I don't want anyone else to know about the Eysen until we understand it."

"Do you remember the part of Clastier's papers where he talks about trust?"

"Yes. He says that trust seems like a never-ending lesson."

"So trust me. Trust Sean."

"Clastier said that in order to understand trust; one must feel betrayal, and then trust again, even knowing that he will be betrayed again."

Gale nodded.

"I can't risk the betrayal."

"But you must."

"Why?"

"Because Clastier told you to and we're dancing in his ballroom."

thirty-five

The FBI Director paced in an open patch of dust between a juniper tree and two large chamisa bushes. "The President and the Attorney General are compliant, but they're also fighting."

"How can they do both?" Barbeau asked.

"Because they have no choice. If they're not compliant, then they're dead. But they are secretly fighting. The trouble is, I don't know if they're patriots or just hungry for their *own* power."

"So, what you're telling me is that we're on our own?"

"No. I'm saying we can't trust anyone but ourselves."

"What about DIRT?"

"DIRT is safe," the Director said. "What about Hall? Do you have any reason to doubt him?"

"Nothing I can think of."

"Just remember, you can't believe anything, not even the truth."

"That kind of makes our job impossible."

The Director looked at Barbeau as if he'd just said something foolish. "Neither the Vatican nor the NSA gets to Gaines before we do."

"Then I need Hall to know."

"Tell him as little as possible. Anyone can be a link back into the administration; anyone can make a mistake and say something, someplace where the NSA has ears."

"We need allies. Isn't there anyone we can join forces with who isn't likely to undercut us?"

"The Attorney General wants the Vatican to get the artifact. The President likely prefers the FBI to win, but he's boxed in ten different ways. The NSA, of course, wants it all to themselves."

"And Booker?" Barbeau asked.

"Booker is a hard one to figure. My guess is, he wants it himself."

"So, he isn't loyal to Gaines?"

"Booker Lipton is only loyal to Ben Franklin," the Director said.

"That seems too easy. Hall thinks there's more to him than that."

"Maybe Hall is working for him."

"Director, not everyone is corrupt."

"It sure as hell feels that way. Speaking of corrupt, then there's our friend, Senator Monroe."

"Where are his loyalties?"

"Barbeau, you've been out in the field too long. Inside the Beltway, most people know that politicians are not loyal. Monroe's a Catholic and the Vatican is a powerful force, their intelligence is already being used to advance him and his policies, and soon it'll discredit his biggest rival, the Governor of Texas. Still, in the end, even the Pope knows that Monroe can't be counted on completely, but they really want another Catholic in the White House. Lest we discount Monroe's ties to the U.S. intelligence community, he's their greatest champion – increasing budgets, expanding powers, and protecting them at every turn. In the end, he'll side with the greatest power."

"Yeah, but is that Booker and his billions, the current President, the Attorney General, the Vatican, or the NSA?"

"Or his ex-girlfriend?"

"Gale Asher has no power."

"Don't be so sure. Monroe has met with Vatican officials, the President, Dover, and the NSA in the last three days. He may not have met with Gale Asher, but don't assume she doesn't count. She already has what everyone else is trying to get."

"So you came to Taos to tell me that the President of the United States is being controlled by the NSA, the United States Attorney General is being controlled by the Vatican, and the man likely to be our next President is frighteningly corrupt?"

"No, I came because we know what Gaines has. The Vatican refers to it as the '*Ater Dies,*' Gaines has dubbed it the 'Eysen' but, regardless this thing is much more than an artifact. It's the history of the planet . . . and its future."

thirty-six

Kruse and Harmer had spent the night in Farmington, New Mexico, awaiting word on their next destination. Booker called just after 7 a.m. local time, to tell them Gaines was at Canyon de Chelly, Arizona, about a three-hour drive.

"It's rugged country and well within the Navajo Reservation, but I did the tribal government a favor a few years back, and I may still have a connection or two there. If we can locate them, we'll need to do an extraction and you should expect competition. I've got a bird on the way and some back-up artillery."

"You're bringing in shooters to take on the feds? Is that the best way to handle this?" Kruse asked.

"It's the only way."

"That sounds less like an extraction and more like an act of war."

"That's just what this is."

Kruse wanted to know where Booker was getting his information. Originally, he'd guessed the source was in the Justice Department, but lately they'd been ahead of the feds. Booker had to have someone inside the administration, possibly the CIA, or maybe even the NSA. But he wouldn't ask, even if the phones had been safe.

Booker would never answer, and would likely fire him for the question.

"We'll be there by ten," Kruse said.

"Good. Hopefully I'll have some new information for you by then." Booker hung up and called the Senator. That Monroe agreed to a second meeting was a good sign. If he'd decided to turn down Booker's billion dollar offer, he could have done that on the phone, but details surrounding a yes, or even a reasonable counter-offer, would require a face-to-face meeting.

As soon as they were finished, Booker would leave the area. No matter what the outcome of their conversation, the nation's capital wasn't safe. Booker was at the center of the greatest crisis in known history, involving only a dozen or so key players. The balance could shift easily with a single death. If a few more died, it was anyone's game.

"Thanks for coming," the Senator said, as they walked through Rock Creek Park near Washington's border with Maryland.

"Have you considered my offer?" Booker asked, stopping along a low bank of river rocks, not far from an old arched stone bridge.

"Yes. But that's not why I asked you here today. Your offer, while generous, falls a little short and I'll have to decline."

"You could have done that over the phone."

"I certainly could have, but as I said; I didn't ask you here to discuss your offer."

"If it's a matter of more money . . . " Booker began.

"No, no. Booker, a billion was a fair amount, even for someone as rich as yourself. But you're competing with the U.S. Treasury and the wealth of the Catholic Church. I'll soon have those at my disposal; so you can keep your money."

"Fair enough, Senator. Then why am I here?" Booker asked, not at all uncomfortable with the blatant corruption contained in the Senator's statement.

"I would like to make you an offer."

"On whose behalf?"

"I'd consider it a personal favor."

Booker hesitated for a moment. He felt certain Monroe would be the next President, knowing better than most that elections didn't mean much, really never did. And he didn't care who occupied the White House. "They're all corrupt," he'd told a friend, who had asked advice on which candidate would be better for his business. "The best one is the one who does what he's paid to do," Booker replied, meaning he paid good money for politicians and expected things in return.

But Senator Monroe was different. Yes, he was shrewd and calculating like all his predecessors, and he even had a decent heart in there somewhere, but each passing year the world consolidated power into fewer and fewer hands, and Monroe was the first to fully understand and have impeccable and strong connections to the three groups that actually run the world – the Church, the corporations, and the Community, also known as the world's intelligence agencies led by the United States.

Monroe could become the most powerful man in history; only one thing stood in his way. Standing there gazing into the eyes of the wildly ambitious Senator, Booker put the pieces together. He often did that during negotiations; all his accumulated wealth was partially owed to his uncanny ability to read people and situations so accurately. The Senator was about to ask Booker's help in obtaining or destroying the only thing that could stop him – the Eysen.

"Tell me, Senator, who would you give it to, if you had it?"

"Give what?" Monroe tried, with his best poker face.

Booker stared unblinking.

"How did you know the favor I would ask?" It was the first time in their negotiations that Monroe had been bested.

"Because, if a man of your power does not want my money; there is only one other thing I might be in the position to do for you."

"Yes, well, you're correct. I'd like your help getting the Eysen from Gaines."

"My question still stands."

"What difference does it make? I might even keep it myself."

"Okay, and what would I get in return?"

"Are you eager to have the Church or the Community as enemies?"

"So, you're threatening me?"

"No, no. It's just that they can be such *good* friends. Surely we all need good friends."

"I have good friends, Senator."

"One can never have too many friends." Monroe smiled.

Booker searched the trees, suddenly worried he might be arrested, or worse. The humidity suggested a thunderstorm. He wore one of his trademark linen suits and carefully took off his jacket, folded it over his arm, and rolled up his sleeves. The Senator watched patiently and loosened his own necktie, thankful for the shade but longing for his air-conditioned car – not far away a driver waited.

"In my experience, friends you have to pay for are worth less than the ones who come free."

"Booker, what do you care about a fancy artifact? Surely, it's not worth going to war over."

"War?"

"Things have been stirred up. Crazy to have all this trouble over something that's been buried forever. Why don't we let the Church and the Community fight over it, and you and I go about our business as usual?"

"You do realize that I don't have it, and don't even know where they are."

"But you might. And if and when you do, I'd like you to cooperate, help me get the Eysen."

"First, tell me who would you give it to, if you had it?"

"The Church."

"Interesting." Booker knew he was lying. He didn't question the Senator's devotion to the Catholic Church; it's just that the smart play would be to give it to the more powerful force; namely, the NSA. But Booker didn't believe Monroe was going to do that either because, with the support he already had from the Church, corporations, and the Community; if Monroe could keep the Eysen for himself, his power would be unmatched and unquestioned. What surprised and worried Booker was that Monroe had already figured that out, and as far as he knew, the Senator had never even laid eyes on it.

"So you'll play ball?" Monroe asked.

"There'll be a price," Booker said, as the two men locked eyes.

"What is it?"

"I'll tell you when the time comes," Booker said, never losing eye contact. "But it'll be a price you're willing to pay."

"Then I can count on you to do the right thing?"

"Senator, when money and power are involved, you can always count on Booker Lipton to do the right thing."

thirty-seven

Sean found Gale and Rip sitting by the stream. The sun filtered through the cottonwood trees, but the canyon's rim was not visible. No one could see them. He watched from a distance for a few seconds before clearing his throat. They were staring at the Eysen, the thing that had caused so much suffering. He wanted to run and grab it, then smash it on the rocks. He would have, too, but it wouldn't bring his brother back; it wouldn't do anything, except prove Josh's death had been a waste. Josh had died guarding that damn thing and no matter what else Sean was going to do, he was determined to protect it.

"Sean, come take a look," Rip said. "You won't believe what incredible things you're about to see."

Sean walked over casually and sat next to Gale. "Keep in mind," she said, "it's eleven million years old."

As Sean gazed inside what appeared to be a crystal ball of impossible age, a thing that ought not to exist, the object responsible for his brother's death, he couldn't help but cry.

Gale put his arm around him. "Who is it?" she asked, already guessing the answer.

"It's my parents, it's me," he said, looking up. "How is this possible? They didn't film it."

"It's your birth?" Gale asked. "How do you know it's not Josh's?"

"I recognize the shirt my dad was wearing from the snapshots, his lucky team jersey. But, I don't understand, no one filmed me being born," Sean repeated.

"We just watched a scene of Rip as a teenager, reading the papers that would lead him to the discovery of the Eysen."

"But how?"

"We don't know," Rip said.

"I thought you said this was a computer," Sean said.

"That's the best way I could describe it before today. Now I don't know what to say." Rip looked back at it. "Jesus!"

"Oh my God," Gale yelled. It showed moving images of Gale, Sean, and Rip huddled around the Eysen, in the exact spots where they now sat. "It's the most remarkable thing I've ever seen. How could it? Rip, how is it doing this? Where is the camera?" She looked up trying to see the camera that was filming them.

Rip stood up and tried to block any incoming signal, all possible camera angles. But the movie continued to show them there, projecting every move they made. "I don't know how it can do this. It must have some kind of reflective camera in there; maybe it uses the curved glass as a lens that's capable of . . . hell, I don't know."

"And what about the footage of you as a teen; of Sean being born? The Eysen wasn't there," Gale said.

Sean had not been expecting anything like this. "This is some kind of UFO, supernatural, sci-fi thing. What's it mean? What else does it show?" Sean swallowed hard. Sweating and nervous, he thought of Busman and what he was supposed to be doing.

Before Rip could answer his question, the Eysen shifted to an aerial view of the Canyon. It was too high up to see any specific movement, but it appeared to be a live moving image of Canyon de Chelly on that day. Sean tried not to panic. He feared that at any moment the Eysen might zoom in on Busman and reveal his betrayal.

"What's it doing now?" Gale asked.

"I don't know," Rip answered. "But Sean, do you see what all the fuss is about? Like I said, even if you don't believe it's millions of years old, how does it do these things?"

"Can it show me my brother's murder? I mean, if it could see me being born; how about Josh being killed?"

Gale looked at Rip. The question had profound implications.

"Why did the Eysen record Sean's birth, Clastier writing his papers, and me reading them as a teenager? All those images are connected to this moment in time," Rip asked.

"Were they the only ones?" Gale asked. "If so, why preserve those times? And if those weren't the only recordings, what else could we see? What, or who, determines which scenes are obtained and stored in the Eysen?"

"Maybe we do," Rip said.

"How?" Sean asked.

"Maybe by our thoughts," Gale said.

"That seems a little far-fetched," Rip said.

"As if the Eysen isn't already very far-fetched. Don't you remember, even back in Asheville, it seemed to answer our questions?"

"Maybe it's voice-activated, but I can't imagine how it could read our thoughts," Rip said.

"But it can film us from above, right now," Sean said softly.

"Yeah," Rip said, looking into the Eysen. The aerial view was shot as if a helicopter were hovering high enough to capture the whole canyon.

"I'd like to see Josh's death," Sean said.

They waited. Nothing happened.

"Maybe *you* have to say it, Rip." Sean looked at him. "Show me my brother's final minutes. Are you willing to do that?"

thirty-eight

Barbeau stared at the FBI Director, trying to understand the implications of his words as the two men stood in the sage and scrub; a hundred and fifty feet away from the Taos headquarters of the New Mexico State Police.

"How can the Eysen be both the history and the future of the planet?" Barbeau's eyes burned, a headache beginning. The gravity of the situation made him worry about his daughter's future. It was the first time his job had made him concerned for her. Perhaps when this ended, he could break away and get out to Los Angeles. Would she be willing to see him?

"DIRT has uncovered information from inside the NSA and Vatican sources. The Eysen is an electronic device."

"So, its purported age is totally invalid?"

"No, we think it is actually eleven million years old."

Barbeau didn't buy it. No one would believe that an electronic device had existed millions of years ago; let alone survived, but it was obvious the Director, the President, the Pope, Booker, and the NSA had all drunk the Kool-Aid, and those folks were all a lot smarter than he was. "No wonder," was all he could say. No wonder everyone was willing to risk everything. If true, a device like that would literally be priceless. The technology alone had to be beyond imagination.

"Yeah. Imagine if a competing nation or our enemies got hold of it," the Director said.

"Imagine if the NSA gets it, that could be just as bad. I'm beginning to believe that the greatest threat to our country is from within the government. Maybe we should let the Vatican have it."

"No. Remember, the people who actually run the Church aren't your friendly neighborhood priests. We have to win this."

"Then what?"

"I don't know. All I can do at this point is figure out a way to beat the bad guys to the prize."

"And do we know who all the bad guys are?"

"Everyone but us."

That sinking feeling returned to Barbeau. He could not dream up a worse situation. What would the classes at the Academy do with this? What would Hall say? Could he even trust him? "We're outgunned," Barbeau finally said.

He replayed the drama of the past week and a half. The case had grown too large, the deaths had mounted, and there were many regrets of what could have been done differently, if he'd only known all this at the start. But investigations didn't work that way; it was one piece at a time, trying to avoid going over a ledge. Damn it, he should have been a park ranger, that's all he ever really wanted, taking care of wildlife, and babysitting happy campers, no stress, no fate-of-the-world on his shoulders. His marriage might have lasted; he would have seen more of his daughter's childhood. Screw it! He should quit right now. Otherwise, he might be dead in a week.

"There's a real chance we won't survive this," Barbeau said, as the Director squatted to inspect an elaborate, red anthill more than three feet in diameter.

"The only way to guarantee our survival is to resign now. I thought a lot about it on the flight. Like you, I've got a family."

"Yeah, well, yours is in a little better shape than mine."

"Maybe so, but do you want them to have a future that is left behind?"

"What do you mean?"

"There are two possible futures. One has freedom expanding. The other takes us back to 1984. The novel, not the year."

"Only worse."

"Yeah, a lot worse. Over the course of history, people have regularly sacrificed themselves for freedom. It's kind of the longest running battle. It's freedom, the ultimate good; repression and control, the beginning of evil. Good versus evil. What do you do, Barbeau? Do you fight? Or are you compliant?"

"This isn't a simple matter. The Church, our President, the Community. I could die and then what?"

"Do you know there are something like twenty thousand different species of ants, an incalculable number of the little buggers, ten billion to the seventh power? A colony can have millions all working for the good of the colony. This one here . . . " the Director pointed at the large hill he'd been watching, "It could have a few hundred thousand ants."

"What's your point?"

"Think about World War II; stopping Hitler was more important than a single life. In fact, the great leaders decided that it was a mission ultimately worth millions of lives. And the people agreed, as millions of them sacrificed their lives to defeat tyranny."

"You're telling me that safeguarding the Eysen is worth my life?"

"I believe it is worth all our lives, as many as it takes."

"And if the Chinese or the Russians find out about it, what will they do for this technology?"

"It was long predicted that World War III would be fought for oil, and recently the Defense Department has shifted its assumptions to disputes over fresh water causing the next major global conflict." The Director shook his head. "But some of our brightest thinkers believe it will be a technology race that will ignite the final war."

"And you think this is the technology?"

"I have no doubt."

"Where's the Director?" Hall asked.

"On his way back to Washington."

"The Director flew two thousand miles, in the middle of the night, just to speak with you for twenty-five minutes?" Hall asked.

"I'll explain on the way. Leave your phone here." Barbeau gave Hall a don't-ask-questions look. Hall checked his phone quickly, and then dropped it on the desk. Barbeau told him the latest intel on the Eysen.

"The Director also brought us a couple of these," Barbeau said, handing Hall a new cell phone. "They're the latest thing – scrambled, untraceable, completely secure."

"Really?" Hall asked, starting to check out the functions. "How long will it take the NSA to crack them?"

"There's a good chance we've got a few weeks, maybe thirty days, before they're compromised. But the truth is, they may already have a way; we have to be careful."

"Can we talk now?"

"Yeah, let's just be careful about what we say and where we say it."

"So, what was his meeting with the President about?" Hall asked, shuffling his stack of photos, which depicted all the parties in the case, so that the President was on top.

"The President and the Attorney General are under extreme pressure. I have no idea how much longer the Director will keep his job. But our bigger problem at the moment, is that the NSA probably already has Gaines."

"In custody?"

"No. As I guessed, they're helping him avoid capture."

"And, do we know why?"

"Because they know what the Eysen is, and they need him to decode it."

"What is it exactly?" He pulled Gaines' photo from the case and studied it.

"It's our new mission. We're to obtain the Eysen at all costs."

"What the hell does that mean? We're Federal law enforcement agents; our job is to investigate crimes and make arrests. Tracking down specific assets that the CIA –"

"We can't trust the CIA."

thirty-nine

The Vatican had nearly two hundred agents working the case from inside the U.S. government. They reported rampant rumors of power struggles and competing interests within the Community. Booker Lipton's name swirled around a long list of potential parties seeking to secure the artifacts.

"How dire is it?" Leary asked Nanski as they ate breakfast from a fast food joint in Gallup, New Mexico. They'd spent the night in another cheap motel room near the Arizona border. Now they waited for a call.

"The object within the bowls, what everyone now refers to as 'the Eysen,' is to the Church, the very embodiment of hell." Nanski downed his remaining orange juice from a plastic cup. "There are those within the U.S. Government who either want it for themselves or, at the very least, don't want us to have it."

"But we have many friends in the government," Leary said. "The Attorney General has assured Pisano they'll turn it over to us."

"That will never happen. While it's true we have friends, there are also countless foreign intelligence operatives who have infiltrated federal agencies. Rome thinks we have only a matter of days before the Chinese, the Russians, and the Israelis get into the hunt. Behind them, Middle Eastern nations, the French, the Germans, and the British; then God forbid if any number of terrorist groups get involved . . . It'll be the end of the world."

"We aren't going to let that happen."

"The Vatican has mobilized at every level; virtually all of their resources around the globe are in this fight, but you and I are on the front lines and unfortunately, as of now, we're nowhere."

"No, we will not lose. God is with us. It doesn't matter if the feds beat us and get this Eysen first. We'll start a holy war to defend our church."

"Harsh words will not get the deed done."

"My words are not empty!" Leary pounded the table. His tin of mints bounced off onto the carpet. "I'm talking about bombing the Capitol building, assassinations, raiding, burning, whatever is necessary. We're a quarter of the world's population. No godless government Bureaucratic greedy scumbags are going to deny the will of God." He stooped to pick up the mints.

Nanski knew Leary meant every word. Extreme didn't begin to describe his views. Normally, that kind of rhetoric made him nervous; might even warrant a report to higher-ups. In this case, it was welcomed because the Church must be saved, and if the Eysen were lost, then a war would be the only hope.

"There is a plan in place. The prophecies have long been clear about the End Times. It is to be a bloody war unlike any other."

"The Vatican has a plan to win World War III?"

"I don't know about winning, but each Pope has lived with the knowledge that the final war will be started by the

Church. The Vatican has a plan to begin it, and a plan to fight it; but winning it, is that even possible?"

"God is on our side," Leary repeated.

"Yes. Let us pray that God helps us win before it has to begin."

"I swear, I'll kill Ripley Gaines when I see him. He works for the devil!"

"Pisano should call any minute with direction."

"God will lead us to Gaines."

"When you're lost in the darkness, you have to believe there is light. Even if you can't see the light, the knowledge that eventually you will; is enough to create the light."

"The Pope?" Leary said, raiding his eyebrows.

"Clastier."

Pisano called, and his news could have been worse. "The NSA is also after the artifacts, and they appear to be close to capturing Gaines, but details are sketchy," he said. "Obviously, if they get the *Ater Dies* before we do; they'll hide it, deny its existence, then dismantle it, in order to learn the technological secrets it holds."

"Not just the tech secrets," Nanski said. "The data it contains would be irresistible to them."

"We need to have faith," Pisano said.

"Faith? Do you really believe the NSA just wants to reverse-engineer this thing to come out with better computers; use the tech to advance the defense industry and communications? And they'll just ignore the contents?" Nanski scoffed at his superior's naïveté. "This is the NSA. They deal in information, using secrets to every advantage. They use intelligence on levels we cannot even imagine."

"Then, get it before they do, because we're running out of time!" Pisano almost screamed over the phone.

"You don't even understand what you just said!" Nanski ended the call and turned to Leary. "The NSA wants the *Ater Dies*, Pisano doesn't get it, but you know what that means, don't you?"

Leary nodded. "Prepare for war."

forty

Barbeau and Hall sat in a small room at the Taos Pueblo Tribal Police station, across from the old Pueblo shopkeeper who had assaulted Gaines. His granddaughter, the tour guide, was also there to be questioned.

"So, you knew Gaines before yesterday?" Barbeau snapped.

Hall couldn't be sure if the shopkeeper was shaking from anger or fear.

"He killed them all," the shopkeeper shouted. "Then, the murdering coward came back here, as if we might have forgotten his crime!"

"Wait, who killed who?" Barbeau asked, not sure how they could have missed another murder in this case.

"Conway," he jammed his finger at the photo of Gaines. "This evil man massacred them in the church!" The shopkeeper grabbed the photo and tore it in four pieces before Hall could grab it.

"My grandfather sees things," the tour guide said. "He sometimes sees several lifetimes at once."

"Like a psychic or something?" Hall asked.

"I don't know what you would call it; he lives in many worlds."

"So, he's crazy," Barbeau said.

"It makes some people crazy, but not him. He is strong; he can see the differences, knows which part goes to which time."

"He doesn't seem to be able to tell the difference between our suspect Gaines and some guy named Conway," Barbeau said.

"They are the same!" the shopkeeper growled.

"Back up. Tell me who Conway is," Barbeau asked.

"Conway was the man who organized and authorized the attack on our church, which resulted in the death of more than one hundred fifty innocent people, who were trapped inside," the tour guide answered.

"When was this?"

"1847."

"1847? So how on earth did Gaines have anything to do with this?" Barbeau asked, incredulous.

"My grandfather believes that Conway has come back as Gaines."

"Reincarnation," Hall said.

"Oh. Kay. Fantasyland, Looney-tunes time," Barbeau said, standing.

"Wait, I don't understand. Why did Conway attack the church?" Hall asked.

"Conway was hunting him," the shopkeeper said, impatiently.

"Hunting who?" Hall asked.

"Clastier!" the shopkeeper said the name as if it should have been obvious.

Hall looked at Barbeau. Supernatural elements aside, he could see the coincidence was too much for a seasoned investigator to ignore. Coincidences almost never are. He'd heard Barbeau once say, "Find enough coincidences and you'll solve any mystery."

Hall was about to say it, but Barbeau got it out first. "Gaines came to Taos for Clastier."

Hall nodded, wide-eyed. "Now that we know why he came here, maybe we can figure out where he went."

"Why is Gaines so obsessed with an ex-communicated priest from the nineteenth century?" Barbeau asked.

"The bigger question might be, why is the Vatican so obsessed with a priest that every Pope for a hundred and seventy years has denied even existed? The questions may start with Gaines, but the answers all end at the Vatican."

They wrapped things up at the Pueblo, leaving with more questions than answers.

"We can't ignore the facts of this case, even if we don't agree with them," Hall said as they drove south.

"What facts am I ignoring?"

"That Clastier and Conway are involved."

"They're dead men! For more than a century!"

"But the fact is, they have come up. And if we don't chase them, we're making a mistake, because Gaines is risking his life to find them."

Barbeau studied a map where he had carefully marked the locations of the Pueblo, San Francisco de Asís, and Chimayó with blue crosses, and a red circle at Grinley's house. He watched the paper as if waiting for something to jump out, a pattern among the lines, sense from the nonsense.

"So, do you know anything about this reincarnation woo-woo garbage?"

"I don't, but my girlfriend is into that stuff. I've also got a niece who wrote a book; she claims was channeled from the other side."

"Yeah, great. But do you know any grown-ups who can help us?"

"They are grown-ups."

"I mean college professors, scientists, qualified people."

"Like the one we're chasing?"

"Gaines? Yeah, he'd be great. Why don't you call Gaines and ask him if he is really a reincarnated mass murderer and, while you two are chatting, invite him to surrender."

They pulled into the shady drive next to Teresa's house. "Now go easy, here," Hall told Barbeau. "This is a sweet little old lady who hasn't done anything wrong."

"Don't worry, I can be a teddy bear when I need to," Barbeau said.

Hall grunted.

Barbeau knocked on the door, "Watch and learn."

The door swung open in an awkward stutter, banging against a wheelchair. Barbeau squinted to see the old woman in the dim light; she appeared frail, wrapped in a worn afghan, head trembling slightly.

"Teresa Mondragon?"

"Who are you?" she shouted, without answering his question. "You can't take my daisies, they're mine!"

"Ma'am, I'm Special Agent Dixon Barbeau and this is Agent Hall. We're with the Federal Bureau of –"

"Turnips, all of ya!"

"Excuse me?" Barbeau turned to Hall, hoping it made sense to him. He shrugged, failing to suppress a smile. Barbeau tried again. "Ma'am, we just have a few questions, do you –"

"The garbage gets picked up on Sundays." She shook a gnarled finger at him. "But, if it rains, leave it there, understand? Dry or wet, smells the same." Teresa spun her wheelchair and slammed the door in one swift motion.

Barbeau pulled his head back to avoid getting hit and then turned to Hall, who couldn't help but laugh. "She's a few gallons short of a full tank."

"Maybe," Barbeau said. "It could also be an act." He pounded on the door. "We could get a warrant," he said to Hall between knocks.

"Why?" Hall asked. "If Gaines was even here, he's long gone."

"But he came for a reason."

"To talk to her? That might not have gone so well."

"My bet is she was lucid then," Barbeau said, just as the door flew open. Suddenly, a hot, red liquid splattered all over him. Teresa flung a now empty pot at him; then slammed the door.

"What the hell!" Barbeau shouted, trying to determine if he'd been hurt. "I'm drenched, what is this?"

"I think it's cherry Jell-O," Hall said, rubbing some on his hands and smelling it.

"She just assaulted a federal agent. I'm going in." Barbeau tried the knob.

"An old lady threw Jell-O at you, hardly an assault."

"No? Next, it may be steak knives or a pistol. I'll bet she's got a house full of guns." The door was locked. Barbeau jogged around back and found a screen door. He peeked inside before pulling it open and drawing his gun. The squeak of antique hinges announced his presence, as he stepped inside the kitchen. A heavy silver tray sailed into his chest from the next room.

By the time the police arrived, Barbeau was bruised and bleeding, and Hall had survived a wild attack from three large, angry cats. Teresa had called the state police to handle the intruders, and for a few tense minutes, Barbeau and Hall were held at gunpoint. Teresa was unharmed, and although she would not be subjected to any questions from Barbeau, she would have to endure a visit from social services to be certain that it was safe for her to continue living alone.

forty-one

Sean and Rip stared at each other tensely. "Show us Josh Stadler's death," Rip finally said, doubting his words could conjure up what Sean so desperately needed to see.

"Someone's coming," Gale said. "A woman on a horse."

Rip looked up alarmed. "It's Mai," he said, relieved and suddenly smiling.

Sean never took his eyes off the Eysen. It continued to show them from above. In it he could see the woman riding up on horseback. The amazing technology could not be as old as Rip had claimed. Sean wished he were smart enough to figure it out, not just the Eysen, but whatever else was going on. The images changed to a swirl and for a moment he hoped, even believed, it might show him Josh's final minutes, but instead it went dark.

"We're going to have to put it away," Gale said.

"No, it's okay. We can trust her," Rip assured.

Both Sean and Gale, for different reasons, were offended at his ease at trusting someone they hadn't met. Neither said anything.

Gale thought Mai looked elegant on the magnificent painted horse, as if she'd ridden out of a dream. When she dismounted and hugged Rip, a little too long, Gale fought against jealousy.

"So, you've returned," Mai said, as the embrace ended.

"This time, I'm the one who needs a favor," he said.

Rip made introductions and Gale thanked Mai for the delicious food.

"You're our guests," Mai said. "It's my pleasure."

"You and Tahoma are saving my life," Rip said.

"That makes me very happy." Mai smiled. "And would you do something for me?" she asked sweetly.

"Name it," Rip said.

"I'd like you to meet someone that I think can help you even more. It's a short walk."

Rip looked to Gale; she shrugged.

"You all are more than welcome to come," Mai said, motioning to Gale and Sean.

Fifteen minutes later, they arrived at an ancient stone dwelling carved out of the cliff in such a way that until one was directly in front of it; it could not be discerned from the natural canyon wall surrounding it. An old Native American man with wrinkled leathery skin, his scraggly gray hair extending half-way down his back, emerged from the structure. His worn denim jeans and thin cotton shirt were the sandy color of the earth. He held two feathers in one hand, and a pouch in the other.

Mai introduced them to Sani-Niyol, which meant "old man of the wind," adding that, in his entire long life, he had never left the canyon. He was like a medicine man or shaman; no one knew how old he was.

"You come from above," Sani-Niyol said to Rip, "to ask questions."

"No. We are," he looked at Mai, "hiding."

"Hiding from answers."

"No, from people," Rip said, unimpressed.

Sani-Niyol stared at Rip for several moments. "They are after you for the answers to the questions you have."

Gale had been fascinated by shamans since doing a story in South America, where she learned that trying to recall later what a shaman had said was not always easy; as if they convey information directly into your subconscious, like a dream. She pulled out a small digital recorder.

Sani-Niyol gently placed an etched hand on the recorder. "This is not needed; it will prevent you from hearing." He moved his fist to his heart. "Listen here; know what is said to you in this way, and all the knowledge of what I say can stay with you."

"It was a pleasure to meet you," Rip said, impatient to return to deciphering the Eysen. "I'm sorry, but we need to get back to work."

Sani-Niyol smiled, brown teeth. "This is part of your work."

"He's right," Gale said. "They're after us for the answers to what the Eysen contains and the meaning of the Sequence."

"Okay," Rip said, turning back to a still-smiling Sani-Niyol. "What should we do?"

Sani-Niyol let his expression go blank and moved his hands slowly in front of Rip's face, as if clearing smoke. "You are lost in fog. It is not clear."

"Why?" Gale asked.

"There is not enough truth around you," he said. "But it will, one day, find you."

Sean remained silent and avoided eye contact with Sani-Niyol.

"What do you mean?" Rip asked.

"If not enough truth is present, then that space fills with deceit, confusion and false signs." Sani-Niyol pulled a stone from his pouch and placed it in Rip's palm. He recognized it as amethyst. "Hold it tightly. It will help with clarity," Sani-Niyol said, brushing feathers down either side of Rip's body. Then he stopped and looked into Rip's eyes. "Conway?"

Gale gasped.

Rip shook his head, and pushed the amethyst back at Sani-Niyol.

"What's wrong?" Mai asked, stopping Rip from leaving.

"Last time a Native American called me Conway, I was beaten, and I wound up running from the cops."

"Rip," Gale said, sternly, "you cannot walk away from this."

"Why did you bring me here?" Rip asked Mai.

"I don't want you to die. Sani-Niyol can help," Mai said. "Is Conway the man after you?"

Rip sighed. "No." He turned back to the old shaman who had stood trance-like since saying the century-and-a-half-old name. "What do you see?"

Sani-Niyol began chanting in an unknown ancient language. Rip looked to Mai. She shook her head, slowly. Two minutes later, the chanting stopped and the old Indian knelt on the ground and began drawing in the dirt.

"This is karma for you," Sani-Niyol said, making a wide figure eight with his finger.

Rip looked puzzled.

"I know you don't believe in past lives," Gale said. "But you're a scientist. Don't deny evidence."

"What evidence?"

"How can you ask that?" Gale asked.

Sani-Niyol stared, glassy-eyed, at Rip. "Remember."

"Remember what?"

"Conway."

"I can't."

"Everything is already known. You can."

Rip shook his head, looked to Mai and shrugged.

"It's not what happened," Sani-Niyol whispered. "It's what you choose to remember. So much is forgotten, that you could say that everything is forgotten. All you must do is remember."

"Clastier talks about reincarnation. How can you not consider it?" Gale asked.

"Because there is no proof. In all of human existence, there is no documented proof of reincarnation."

"How do you document such a thing?" Gale asked. "And what about Clastier?"

"No one is right about everything. Not even Clastier."

"What about the Divinations? They've all come true. And you found the Eysen."

"I've already told you; parts of Clastier's papers never made sense to me."

"Yet, you blindly followed the other parts, why?"

"I don't know," Rip said, quietly.

"There had once been a door," Sani-Niyol interrupted.

"What?" Rip asked.

"Sani-Niyol has traveled between the worlds," Mai said.

"What door? Where?" Rip asked.

"It is lost," Sani-Niyol said, sadness filling his face.

"I'm sorry, Mai," Rip said, "but this is all too much of a distraction. We've got some very nasty people after us. I've got to figure out these artifacts and keep moving."

"Conway. You must remember, Conway," Sani-Niyol said, grabbing Rip's arm. "You knew."

"Knew what?" Rip asked, trying but unable to pull his arm away.

"You knew it was wrong." The old man stared deeply into his eyes. "You must remember, Conway," he repeated. "It was wrong."

Rip couldn't shake his grip or his gaze. The same dizzy sense of *déjà vu* he'd experienced at the churches swirled in his head. He felt drunk and fell to his knees. Suddenly, he was overtaken by the emotions of a scared and angry man named Conway.

"I did know it was wrong," Rip said weakly. "I knew, but I chased him anyway."

Sani-Niyol closed his eyes causing Rip to fall flat on the ground.

Gale and Mai went to help him up, but Sani-Niyol held out his hand to stop them. He chanted more incomprehensible words.

Rip staggered to his feet, sand clenched in his fists.

"What happened?" Gale asked.

"I was Conway. I knew the Church was wrong, but I wanted to kill Clastier and destroy his papers."

"Why?"

"I don't know," he said, turning back to Sani-Niyol.

"Trust the deepest part of yourself . . . the part that knows everything."

"How?"

Sani-Niyol bore his eyes back into Rip's, answering silently. Rip understood. His eyes welled with tears. The old man turned, resumed chanting, and walked away.

forty-two

Mai did not return to their camp. None of them was very talkative, and dutifully resumed their studies. As the Eysen woke up, Gale gasped.

"That's me in Peru!"

"When?" Rip asked.

"About five years ago, I was there on a story for National Geographic."

"Machu Picchu?"

"No, the Nazca Lines. But that trip was a turning point in my life. I had just turned thirty and had really begun to question my own spirituality, past lives, my purpose, the universe, all that."

"Peru will do that to people, but generally, they get home and return to their senses," Rip said.

"How does it know this stuff?" Sean asked. "My birth, you as a teenager, and now Gale in Peru? What does it mean?"

"It's like it knows who we are." Gale said.

"I know," Rip said. "How advanced was the society that created these things?"

"Things? There's more than one?" Sean asked.

Gale and Rip exchanged a glance. "The casing, the Eysen, and this." Rip pulled out the small stone Odeon with the matching gold inlaid bands.

"What's that?" Sean asked.

"It was found with the Eysen. We have no idea what it is or if it does anything." Rip wasn't comfortable with anyone else knowing that there was another Eysen. Gale's expression told him she didn't agree with keeping information from Sean, but she kept quiet.

"If these artifacts are as important as you say, why did you waste all that time going to Catholic churches?" It was a question Busman had wanted him to ask. "I mean you claim the Vatican killed Josh; wouldn't you want to avoid them? Shouldn't you have been hiding?" Busman didn't want him to keep bringing up Josh, but knew he would; it was the reason for his cooperation.

This time Gale got words out first. "The churches, the Eysen, and Josh's death are all connected. The first time we were able to work with the Eysen for more than an hour, it showed us a priest named Clastier."

"Gale," Rip said, in a sharp tone and hard eyes.

She ignored him. "Clastier lived in northern New Mexico two hundred years ago," Gale said, making sure not to look at Rip. "The leaders of the Catholic Church ordered him killed."

"Why?"

"In part because he predicted the Eysen would be found. It was his papers that led Rip to make the discovery."

"So you're telling me that the Vatican has been killing people in order to suppress this thing for centuries?" Sean asked.

Gale nodded.

"Why? What are they afraid of?"

"The same thing people are always afraid of," Rip said.

Sean stared at him, waiting.

"People are really only afraid of two things . . . the unknown and the truth."

"I thought it was death," Sean said.

"Death is the great unknown," Rip said.

"I'm not going to debate this with you; I get enough of that with my philosophy professor. I'm just curious as to why you think the most powerful religion in the world has spent centuries trying to stop this."

"My guess is for both reasons: they don't want the truth to come out, because it will invalidate their version of the world; and they're terrified of the unknown. They're afraid to find out who created such a thing . . . and why?"

"But how could your priest have known?" Sean asked.

"It's eleven million years old, so stories of it may have come down through myth and legend, maybe divine guidance. Clastier was a prophet," Rip said.

"Divine guidance? Why would the Church fear something that came through divine guidance?" Sean asked.

"The Vatican believes that they are the one true Church; that they alone interpret the meaning and message of the one true God. What if they're wrong? What if Catholicism is built on a flawed foundation?" Rip said.

"They've killed everyone who's seen it," Gale said. "It's probably something none of us knows. Maybe something in the missing Clastier Papers."

Rip, surprised by her theory, and upset at her mention of the missing Clastier Papers in front of Sean, tried to change the subject. "We don't know anything for sure, just that the Eysen is extraordinary and we must protect it."

Sean's expression remained skeptical. "You say it's eleven million years old. How could it be?"

"I don't care if you believe it's that old," Rip said. "I'm not trying to prove it to you. But regardless of its age, its technology is far beyond anything we're even close to in our *advanced* world."

"How can an archaeologist, of all people, believe this thing is even more than ten years old?"

"Why are you so angry? Every conversation with you is a fight," Rip said. "You can't keep blaming me for your brother's death."

Sean's jaw clinched, his eyes narrowed.

"I accept responsibility for sending him on the errand that got him killed," Rip continued. "But I had no idea he was in danger of anything more than being arrested."

"Yet, you claim the Church murdered him and has already killed people for the Eysen."

"But, I didn't know that then."

"You knew about Clastier; he led you to the Eysen. You said they tried to kill him."

"Damn it, Sean, that was a hundred and fifty years ago. How could I know they were still pursuing this?"

"You knew."

forty-three

Sean took a walk to cool off. It was Gale's suggestion and he didn't need much convincing. As much as he tried to get along with Rip, it was impossible. Fifteen minutes away from their camp, he climbed a sloping cliff, until he reached the high point where the NSA-issued mini-sat phone found a signal. The ledge made him a little nervous; he'd never been good with heights, but it was the closest place he'd found where the phone worked. Sean gave his report.

Busman had been exercising and was breathing fast. "Are you keeping your cool?" he asked, knowing Sean's psychological profile and the pressure he faced.

"I've got it under control." Sean's lie concerned Busman.

"Listen, Sean, I'm counting on you. We've gone to a lot of trouble to put you in this position. If you don't come through, then I can't keep up our end of the bargain. Gaines has information that we need and you have to get it. We're working on getting live monitoring set up at your camp, but that likely won't be in place until the morning. So, in the meantime, don't push too hard. We want Gaines to stay right where he is until we get everything we need."

"What if he decides to go?"

"He'd be making a mistake. Gaines will not leave the canyon with those artifacts."

"Okay."

"Make sure you're his best friend, understand?"

"Yeah, I got it. I'll be cool."

"Good." Busman resumed cycling on his portable stationery bike.

Sean walked back to the camp, looking around nervously, worried the "Indians" were watching him. The paranoia, grief, and guilt were choking. "Best friend," Sean said to himself, just before he reached the camp. "Josh was my best friend."

Sean panicked when he saw Tahoma whispering to Rip over near the creek. Tahoma nodded toward Sean. The two of them stopped talking and walked over to him. Gale sat next to the Eysen, near the tent.

"Sean, Tahoma needs to show me something a few miles' ride from here. We'll be back before nightfall," Rip said.

"Fine, I'll hang out here with Gale," Sean said, relieved he hadn't been found out.

"I want Gale to come with us," Rip said, now standing in front of Sean.

"Why can't I come?" he asked, suddenly suspicious again.

"I just think some time alone will do you good. We'll be back soon."

"Why do I need time alone?" Sean said, agitated.

"Look, man, I know you're still trying to cope with your loss and –"

"My loss? My loss! How about trying to deal with the fact that you killed my brother!" Sean yelled.

Rip looked over at Gale, searching hard for patience. Wanting to tell her, "I told you so," he took a deep breath. "Sean, once again, I'm sorry, I asked Josh to take the casing. But the Vatican killed him, not me."

"Lies. All you say is lies. You killed Josh!"

"What are you talking about?" Gale asked. "Sean, please, I miss him too, but you have to stop blaming Rip."

"He's going to kill you next and then me. That's what he does!"

"Calm down," Rip said. "You're talking crazy."

"You calm down. You're the crazy killer."

"Sean, I was with you when Josh was killed!" Rip yelled. Tahoma put a hand on Rip's shoulder.

"You didn't want to get your *important* hands dirty, but you killed him. It still counts; even if you have someone else do it!"

"Sean, you're upset. Not only would it have been impossible for Rip to kill Josh, but he had no reason to kill him," Gale said.

"They showed me a video! I saw him pay the killers. He looked at photos of my dead brother and then paid the killers cash."

Gale and Rip looked at each other, stunned.

"Who?" Gale asked.

But Rip had already figured it out. He began scanning the area, trying to see up to the rim. Someone had gotten to Sean and convinced him that Rip had killed Josh.

"He's a plant. They know we're here!" Rip yelled.

Sean ran at Rip, fists swinging wildly. One of them connected on the side of Rip's face, knocking him down. Tahoma shoved Sean backwards. He stumbled and then took off, running. Gale clutched the Eysen. Tahoma helped Rip to his feet.

"Damn it! After all this and we're done in by a kid. One of our own!" Rip shook his head and shot a seething look toward Gale.

"I can't believe he did this. I'm sorry, Rip," Gale said breathlessly, as she grabbed her things.

Rip couldn't bring himself to answer. He hadn't wanted to trust Sean, but he'd never imagined this. In confused panic, he took the Eysen from Gale, ran to the tent, got his pack, and checked the gun. Ready to go, he called to Tahoma. "We need to get out of here." Then looked around. "Gale, where's Tahoma?"

"I don't know," she said. "He must have gone after Sean."

"Tahoma," he yelled.

Gale ran through the trees to look farther down the canyon.

"We have to find him; he's our ticket out of here," Rip said, chasing her. "The feds could be here any minute."

"Who do you think got to Sean?"

"Does it matter? Whoever it is wants to kill us."

forty-four

Kruse and Harmer had spent the day driving around the rim, stopping at overlooks, and trying to look like tourists. With high-powered binoculars and GPS, they searched methodically, hoping to get lucky and catch a glimpse of something down in the canyon that would lead them to their target. Booker checked in twice but still had no new leads.

They expected additional personnel to arrive at any time. AX, Booker's large and secret security force, had an elite division known as Black-AX, or BLAX, that was populated by former special ops soldiers. A BLAX crew was called in only when Booker found himself in particularly sticky situations. This was clearly one of those times.

NSA operatives surrounded them, the FBI couldn't be far behind, and lethal Vatican agents were God knows where. Booker had an interest in Gaines and the objects he held; and had shown a fearless disregard for the law in protecting that interest.

Kruse had worked with BLAX in North Africa, when terrorists had unknowingly tangled with a Booker company, and he welcomed their help here. The only chance to extract Gaines would be by using extreme tactics and highly trained personnel. "The Vatican boys might be hoping for divine intervention," he told Harmer, "I'm counting on BLAX."

Barbeau rode back to Taos, sticky and wet from Teresa's Jell-O attack. Hall continued to tease him, especially when he saw how angry it made him. Once Barbeau got cleaned up, back at their motel, his spirits improved slightly.

"I'm telling you, she wasn't crazy," Barbeau repeated. "I want to talk to her again."

"Now who's crazy?" Hall laughed, as they got in the car to head back to the state police headquarters. "And you say, 'talk to her again?' I don't recall her doing much talking with you. All I remember is her whipping your ass!"

"Yeah, well, maybe this time you should go in first, tough guy."

"And risk getting pelted with marshmallows? No sir." Hall couldn't stop laughing. "You go alone. I'll be here writing up the report: 'decorated federal agent pulls gun on hundred year-old woman serving Jell-O.' Lucky she didn't use something really dangerous like vanilla pudding!"

A DIRT agent was waiting in the parking lot and got out of his car as they parked. He handed Barbeau a file on the Eysen. He flipped through it briefly. "Where did you get all this?"

"The NSA isn't the only one who can intercept and unscramble," the agent said proudly.

"This came from the NSA?" Barbeau asked.

"Primarily. We did get a few additional details from the only person, outside of Gaines, Asher, and Sean Stadler; who has seen it . . . and is still alive."

"Who?" Hall asked.

"Grinley."

"You found Grinley?" Barbeau asked.

"Alive?" Hall asked.

"Yes to both."

"Can we talk to him?"

"I'm afraid he's in protective custody. The Director believes the Vatican has a kill order on him. The NSA isn't likely to bring him flowers either."

"Where?"

"We've got him in a safe house in Colorado, but we're moving him again today."

"I need to talk to him," Barbeau said.

"Take it up with the Director."

"When am I going to talk to him next?"

"I'm not sure. In the meantime, read the report and I'll pass along your request."

"I'd like to plead my own case to the Director. Grinley is critical to the investigation."

"I'll convey your concerns. Now, we have reason to believe Gaines is on his way to Flagstaff, Arizona."

"His father?" Hall asked.

"Yes."

"He wouldn't be that dumb," Hall said. "He has to know that a hundred people with guns are waiting there for him."

"Gaines is not dumb, he's a genius, and smart people always do dumb stuff because they believe they're so smart," Barbeau said.

"Sometimes," the DIRT agent added, "they simply run out of alternatives. A man without choices is usually the most dangerous."

"Gaines is not a man without choices," Hall said. "He's the guy holding all the cards."

"Let's hope he's at least a patriot and not one of Booker's properties. I'd hate to see that thing sold to the highest bidder."

They read the report in nearby Red Willow Park. "Can you believe this thing?" Barbeau said. "Last night I finished Gaines's manuscript, *The Future of the Past*, and I have to admit, he may have proven his Cosega theory."

"If the Eysen really is an eleven-million-year-old computer, he's proven a lot more than the Cosega theory."

"So, it's clear the Vatican sees this as a threat to their Church doctrine, but they've had threats before. Isn't that what they say faith is all about? They can pray away anything that doesn't agree with their version of the world. Why does this one warrant such a massive response?" Barbeau asked.

"The Vatican has Attorney General Dover in place and soon they'll have the President of the United States, assuming Monroe gets elected."

"That hardly seems in question."

"So, for the first time in the modern era, at least since Kennedy, and on a much grander scale; the Pope will actually be the de facto leader of the world, albeit behind the scenes."

"And the Eysen is the only thing that could stop this from happening?"

"World domination seems as good a reason as any to kill a few dozen non-believers."

forty-five

In Flagstaff, Arizona, Nanski and Leary arrived at the radio station where Rip's father worked. They knew a lot about the senior Mr. Gaines. An extremely conservative Republican who, although not Catholic, attended an Episcopal church religiously. That was close enough for Nanski, although Leary still considered him a heathen. They sat in the parking lot, listening to Gaines' father espouse upon many of their own beliefs during his talk show. Leary couldn't fathom how such a man would allow his son to grow up and destroy the world.

"He's not too close with his son, but the professor may have no other options," Nanski said.

"A team has already bugged his house, phone, and office. If his son contacts him, we'll know. We even have his father's favorite coffee shop being watched." Leary smiled.

"We need an update from the Attorney General. What does the FBI have?" Nanski asked. "Gaines could be anywhere by now. What if he's nowhere near Arizona?"

"The FBI is a joke." Leary sneered. "Gaines has been lucky, but the oldest and mightiest power on earth is about to smear this bug on its windshield."

Nanski envied Leary's blind faith, but he knew that most battles were lost while the losers clung to their faith that they would be won. "And what if God's will is for Gaines to escape?" Nanski asked. "Where do the prophecies come from?"

"Clastier? He was an agent of Satan," Leary blasted.

"And *Saint* Malachy?"

"They are fakes!"

"They are not," Nanski said, calmly.

"I too am a prophet, hear my words," Leary shouted, raising his arm above his head. "Gaines will fail. It is known unto me, for it will be my hand that ends his life." Leary dropped his voice to a whisper "God has chosen me for this purpose, have no doubt. Whatever quest Gaines thinks he's on will end very soon."

Nanski nodded, but was no less worried.

On the short plane flight to Flagstaff, Barbeau and Hall continued their conversation. The Eysen report had shaken them both. For the first time, they fully understood what they were dealing with; that missing piece which had eluded and bothered them throughout the case, now had finally fallen into place. The report terrified them with its implications.

"What do you think the NSA is planning to do with the Eysen?" Hall asked.

"Assuming they get it before we do?" Barbeau asked.

"Or before the Vatican."

"They'll use the technology for national security. I imagine that will eventually extend into aerospace, defense, Silicon Valley, and, depending on the contents, maybe even into pharmaceutical and medical applications."

"And a potential boon for the U.S. economy."

"Sure, but there'll be a dark side, too. There always is," Barbeau said. "The NSA could completely monitor every single aspect of our lives, leading us farther down the Orwellian path. First it'll be in the name of national security. Then, when too much power is concentrated in too few hands, this new technology will help quash dissenting voices, and eventually 'the elimination of all threats domestic or otherwise' is going to have a very broad definition."

"Quite a rosy picture," Hall said.

"Yeah, it's already happening. Guys like you and me, we see the crime and the worst of society, so it's easy to rationalize bending the rules, but slowly the things that made this country great are being chipped away."

"So you think it's inevitable, even without the Eysen?" Hall asked.

"The fact is nobody other than Gaines really knows what he really has in those artifacts. All the stuff in this file is conjecture, pieced together on the fly."

"You read the section about the Vatican; it sure seems like they have seen the Eysen. And if he's got what they say, then it's the key," Hall said.

"The key to what? The road to ruin or the path to redemption?"

"I don't know. But what if . . . " Hall said, leaning close to Barbeau. "What if his find could be used for good instead of evil and control? It could have all the answers. Maybe the Eysen contains the miracle of peace and mindfulness, sustainable energy, health, everything."

"What if that scares us so much that we destroy it?"

"Who would do that?"

"The Pope, the President, this one, or the next . . . maybe a unit manager within the NSA. What about the Director? He knows how dangerous it would be if the wrong people got the Eysen, and if we do our job, the opportunity will be all his. After reading this report, I'm not sure I'd blame him."

"And Gale Asher's relationships with Monroe and Gaines make her a real wild card."

"Booker, too. His reputation for being fiercely loyal is a plus for Gaines, but the Eysen is too valuable and may trump everything."

"My guess is that Booker has known all along what he's been hoping to find. Just look at Gaines's career, funded primarily by Booker, and a single-minded obsession toward Cosega . . . the Eysen. Booker has loyalty, all right, but it ain't to Gaines, it's to power."

DIRT, the Director's secret team, had approved field agents on the case who met and briefed Barbeau at the airport.

"We seem to be watching Vatican agents, watching Gaines's father at his residence, and at the radio station," the DIRT agent said. "We did get a listening device onto the Vatican agents' car at the residence."

"Excellent." Barbeau said, looking at Hall. It had been Hall's idea, and DIRT had facilitated the equipment and monitoring. They'd put a bug on Nanski and Leary's vehicle while they were briefly held at Chimayó. Those tactics and the results they had yielded so far had been kept from the Attorney General. The Director had authorized rounding up all known Vatican agents if necessary, but full DIRT surveillance had proven to be even more effective.

DIRT had made incredible progress in the case. The Eysen report and an ongoing investigation into Dover, the President, and Booker had impressed Barbeau so much that he'd told Hall that if the Director held onto his post after this case, Barbeau was planning on requesting a transfer to the elite unit.

Hall didn't tell Barbeau, but he fully expected that before the case was resolved that the Director, Barbeau, and he would all be dead.

forty-six

Gale and Rip ran for ten minutes, but there was no sign of Tahoma or Sean.

"We can't keep running; they could be anywhere," Gale said, stopping to catch her breath.

"Tahoma is our only chance to escape before the damn helicopters come!"

"Maybe we should start yelling for him."

"And what if the FBI or the Vatican agents hear us?"

"If they're that close, we're dead anyway."

"Right." Rip cupped both hands around his mouth and yelled, "Tahoma, Tahoma."

"The canyon walls just swallow the sound," Gale said. "Why don't we split up? I'll go up here and you go that way."

"Okay," Rip said, walking away. Then, realizing there was the possibility they might never see each other again, he stopped. "Good luck . . . you know, in case something happens."

"You, too." She turned before he could see her tears. Gale was touched that he said goodbye, especially after Sean turned out to be a traitor. She felt awful for championing him. Her intuition had missed on this one, clouded by the guilt she felt because of Josh's death. Rip's instincts had been right, but he'd ignored them for her. "How has it come to this?" Gale asked, turning to Rip, but he was gone. She was alone.

Rip continued calling for Tahoma, and a few minutes after leaving Gale, his friend responded. "Rip, over here."

"Where?"

"Here." Tahoma stood up and Rip saw him off to his left about forty feet ahead. He reached him seconds later and found Tahoma crouching over Sean. "He's dead."

Sadness filled Rip and it took several moments to manage some words. "What happened?"

"He was climbing the canyon wall there," Tahoma motioned. "I yelled for him to stop. When he heard me, he turned and shouted something, then lost his footing and fell."

"Oh, God. How high up?"

"Maybe twenty feet. He was trying to call someone." Tahoma handed Rip Sean's NSA phone.

"Did he complete the call?"

"He could have. I'm not sure."

Rip tried to check, but the phone had been badly damaged.

"Two brothers dead. One day, I'll have to see their parents and try to explain all of this." Rip shook his head. "How am I going to do that?"

"We need to go or you'll never get that chance. If he got that call off, then we're already too late."

Rip shook his head, taking one last look at Sean. "Will you come back for his body?"

"Of course." Tahoma looked around marking the location in his mind. "Where's Gale?"

"We split up, hoping to find you faster."

"Never a good idea to split up," Tahoma said.

That's when they heard the helicopter.

"Follow me!" Tahoma grabbed Rip, practically dragging him along an ancient trail, hidden amongst the boulders near the cliff.

"What about Gale?"

"We can't risk it now. She could be anywhere."

Rip knew he had to protect the sphere, but the thought of Gale's getting caught sickened him.

An hour later, they found Mai at a small stable where horses were kept for guided rides with tourists. "There hasn't been another flyover. I'll go back and find Gale. Mai will get you out on horseback."

"Horseback?"

"Do you want to chance the road?"

"No," Rip said.

"There's only about an hour of daylight left," Mai said. "We'll be doing the steeps in the dark." She looked at Tahoma.

"It's a clear night and there'll be a moon. He can do it." He looked at Rip.

"I'll just follow Mai."

"The horse knows the way," she said.

"If I find Gale in time, we'll meet at Tension Rock," Tahoma said, as he started back the way they'd come.

"If he finds Gale?" Rip said to Mai.

"Don't worry, Rip, it's a big canyon, but Tahoma knows it well."

He looked at the horse and then up the steep canyon, wondering where there was a trail that a horse could navigate . . . in the dark. Then a bigger fear entered his mind. Maybe they hadn't heard another helicopter because they'd already gotten Gale. "She would have told them I was somewhere else," he thought. "She sacrificed herself to save me and the Eysen, and I've abandoned her."

forty-seven

"Find out who the hell is flying that bird," Busman barked to a subordinate. The NSA had forty agents blending in with summer tourists around the area. "That son of a bitch may have just blown our cover." It seemed inconceivable to him that a helicopter would come out of nowhere and buzz the canyon. No great military leader he'd ever read about would make such an idiotic miscalculation. There must be a civilian there to help Gaines.

It had been Booker's pilot who had made a mistake by flying over the canyon. Behind schedule and ferrying additional AX agents, he did not understand the sensitivity of the mission.

Harmer had been searching the canyon with binoculars, while Kruse had been scanning through his sniper's scope. They were shocked when the chopper appeared. Kruse immediately called Booker to complain. "This is no small error. Rip is going to assume the chopper belongs to the feds. He'll run before we can get to him."

"I know, damn it. And the NSA is going to launch into a full scramble over this. They may just scoop him up; knowing someone else is this close. You've got to find him."

"We've been trying."

"Not hard enough," Booker said. "The FBI and the Vatican boys are already in Flagstaff. Even the NSA won't be able to protect Gaines if he drives into that trap."

"All we can do is work the rim with the extra manpower that's arrived, and hope we catch him coming out of the canyon," Kruse said, waving off Harmer's cigarette smoke.

"And if he stays put?" Harmer asked, listening to Kruse's side of the conversation.

"She's right," Booker said. "Get a couple guys into the canyon."

"It's more than one hundred thirty square miles in rugged unfamiliar terrain. We couldn't adequately cover that with one hundred men. The rim alone is nearly forty miles around and, need I remind you, the entire area is within, and subject to the laws of the Navajo Nation. We should stay on the rim for a few hours in case we get lucky, and then work the routes to Flagstaff."

Booker respected and sought employees who were not afraid to speak their minds. Kruse was right and he believed that Gaines was too smart to stay in the canyon; even if the helicopter hadn't shown up. The FBI would eventually cross check all his past digs in the southwest, and overlay it with all the roads leading out of Española, if they hadn't already. From there, a list of known associates would eventually lead them to Tahoma. Booker, a step ahead, already had somebody on the way to talk to Tahoma. If not for the helicopter screw-up, they would have had Gaines in the next few hours.

"Okay, get AX all over the rim, near any possible exit points. And remember, they could be on foot, horseback, motorcycles, who knows," Booker said.

"He's friendly with the local Navajo. This area is filled with caves and concealed passages that he could slip through undetected or use as a hiding place."

"I'll see what I can find out. The person Rip trusts most inside the Navajo Nation owes me a favor."

forty-eight

The stable had six horses. Mai saddled the two best. "Have you ridden since the last time we were together?" she asked.

"No, I'm sorry to say. Good memories," Rip said, feeling awkward.

She steadied the horse while he mounted. "She's gentle and will carry you, don't worry," Mai said. He loved animals, was even a decent rider, but the horse did not seem gentle. She felt angry and powerful under Rip. The trail would be treacherous.

"Yours is called Rain," Mai said, swinging into her saddle. "She is determined; don't confuse that with anger."

"Okay, Rain," Rip said quietly to his horse. "I need your help."

Rain galloped away, following Mai's horse. Rip hung on. Occasionally they heard engines, but the echoes between canyon walls made distances and sound directions impossible to gauge. Rip wondered how long it would take for the helicopters to return.

"Now I know how Clastier felt when I was chasing him two hundred years ago," he thought. Clastier had written about being trapped in a canyon, pursued by a posse, which would have included Conway. Rip realized that, after talking to the old shaman the day before, he might have been Conway. He was too afraid to admit it to Gale, or even to himself. The Eysen had taught him that anything was possible and everything could be something else. He wished he knew what had happened to Clastier.

"Choices always have messages," Mai said, breaking the trance of hooves on rocky ground and the labored breathing of horses.

"Why are we stopping?" He had hardly been aware of their slowing down.

"There are two ways up from here. One is longer and will take most of the night, but it is much easier."

"And the other?"

"Horribly steep, but shorter."

"There'll be more helicopters soon. We have to get out," Rip said. "And the longer it takes, the more time they have to fill the canyon with agents who might find Gale."

"This way then," she said. He followed as the nearly invisible trail immediately started to climb. "Gale is a beautiful woman."

Her comment caught Rip by surprise. He grunted some sound that could be construed as agreement and hoped the conversation would go no further.

"Do you love her?"

"Who?"

Mai laughed. "So the answer is yes."

"Look, Mai, my nerves are frazzled and any minute I could be shot out of this saddle. Do you mind if we don't talk about such trivial matters?"

"Ha! Since when is love a trivial matter?"

"I walked into that one, didn't I?" Rip asked, as the horse negotiated a tight switchback and he was surprised that he was already peering down a thirty-foot drop.

"You have only known her a short time; as I recall, that's when you fall the hardest."

"Mai, we were different. I could not stay and you could not leave."

"Would not stay, would not leave."

"Semantics," Rip said tentatively, as his horse rounded another turn and he teetered in the saddle.

"Regardless, it was a timing issue. You may have the same thing with this one."

"Seriously, can we talk about something else?"

"We're two former lovers fleeing a sacred canyon on horseback in the dark of night. I can think of nothing better to talk about unless you'd prefer to talk about Conway." Mai laughed.

"I never said I loved Gale," Rip said. "Anyway, I never got over you."

"How could you have? You knew me only in sunsets, flower blossoms, and starlight on the river."

"Ah yes, I remember it well."

"And we played at all this while working among the origin-artifacts of my people . . . which you discovered . . . and then the drama of the battle to save them."

"I tried to do the right thing."

"You did, Rip. You did the right thing returning the Navajo artifacts; you traded your passion for Cosega for *our* passion. I know what that took. And your gesture almost drew me into your world, but you know this place holds too much mystery and magic to surrender to the pretend-world, where the majority of white people live."

"You and Gale have that in common – the dream that there is something more, as if we could just lift a veil."

"The veil flutters open all the time, and most people look the other way. But you do something worse."

"What's that?"

"You close your eyes."

"Oh, really."

"If you didn't, you would have stayed in Canyon de Chelly with me. You wouldn't have been able to ignore those feelings."

"Me, without my work; isn't me at all."

"You could have worked from here. Where do you live now, all alone in West Virginia somewhere? I would have waited."

"Let's talk about Conway, instead."

"Okay."

"No. I'm really just trying to change the subject."

"I know you are. But don't worry; we've got hours ahead and I intend to cover it all."

forty-nine

They rode in silence until their horses trotted to a stop.

"Why are we stopping?" Rip asked.

Mai pointed ahead. In the final light of dusk, nothing resembling a path for people, let alone a horse, was visible.

"Where's the trail?" Rip asked, confused.

"Right there." Mai nodded toward what to Rip looked like a wall above them.

"I guess we leave the horses here."

Mai dismounted. With barely enough room to maneuver, she reached into a saddle bag and pulled out a handful of dried herbs, held them out to Rain, and then put her face against the horse's and whispered some Navajo words. She carefully placed blinders on Rain and then repeated the same procedure with her horse. "They *will* go," she said, swinging herself back up into the saddle.

Rip, astonished, looked up into the darkness above. All he could make out was the shadowy outlines of steep craggy rocks and outcrops. "Have they ever done this before?"

"Not in this lifetime," Mai said, kicking her horse. "Haaw!"

Her horse lurched forward and Rain followed. He held on tight and for a few harrowing minutes forgot about helicopters and Vatican agents. They rode fast; he slipped but caught himself before going off Rain's back. The night made it hard to tell just how much ground they covered before the horses found a twenty-inch wide trail on the edge of a cliff. Too dark to see the bottom, which he knew to be hundreds of feet straight down, Rip kept his eyes on Mai's back, her long black hair, swinging softly from side to side. He missed the feel and the smell of it.

"Is the worst behind us now?" he asked.

"We have a couple of more rough spots ahead, but not much worse."

"Splendid."

Mai laughed. "We'll be all right." Then she was quiet. "I confess, I was wrong."

Rip wasn't sure he heard her. "What?"

"I should have convinced you to stay. You would have, I knew it then. There was that moment during our last night together when the monsoon finally let up and we walked outside to feel the humid air, to smell the moisture on the desert."

"I remember."

"Of course, you recall the night, but do you remember *the* moment?"

"I do. We were wrapped in nothing but those beautiful blankets your grandmother made and you convinced me to put them down on the wet muddy ground. Stars poked through the retreating clouds, and . . . that warm breeze and our endless embrace."

"That's it. That's when I should have asked you to stay. You would have, wouldn't you?"

"In that moment, I would have done *anything* for you, Mai."

"Then why didn't you tell me then?"

"Fear."

"What were you afraid of?"

"You."

"Me? I loved you."

"I know. That's what scared me." Rip appreciated the darkness between them; discussing his feelings had never been easy. Somehow, with his life threatened, and riding a horse on the edge of a cliff made it easier, but being invisible in the blackness of the night helped most of all. "I love you, Mai. But I'm not as good as you. You have some pure streak of love that I've never experienced before. I feel as if I'm dreaming you. Like when we're together, we don't need anything. We could just melt into that warm breeze on that muddy ground and forget the world."

"We could."

"I know we could, but I can't accept that kind of happiness. I'm chasing something."

"You could have chased it from here; you could have done it with me."

"No. I don't have a pure streak of love inside me. I've got a burning, painful sadness."

"Why?" Mai's voice was strained.

"I don't know."

"Let me help."

"All I can tell you is, it's always been there, and the first time I ever felt the pain diminish was when I pulled the Eysen from that limestone in Virginia. That's when I realized that it wasn't something people could fix for me, but at the same time, I wasn't permanently defective. Cosega hadn't made me that way; Cosega was the cure!"

"For what? Your karma?"

"I don't know. For years I felt this discontentment, something missing, something really big. Like, why does everyone else seem happy, when there are all these holes in me?"

"And the Eysen has filled that?"

"Maybe not filled it yet, but it's shown me the answers exist." As the horses cautiously navigated the edge, Rip looked up at the night sky. The Navajo Nation was one of those rare spots on earth where the stars were so numerous that it appeared the sky might collapse from their weight. "If I had stayed with you, Mai, you would have been miserable; maybe having caught my tragic melancholy. I couldn't stand to watch that glow of yours extinguished, and to be the cause of it . . . that would have killed me."

"How do you know that you wouldn't have absorbed some of my 'glow,' or what if we defeated your problems together?"

"I wish you understood. It's my fault for not being able to explain. I swim in sadness and loss. Ever since I was a kid, I've felt pain, even when laughing," Rip said, frustrated. "But you know I would have gone just as crazy on the reservation as you would have living off of it."

"I know," Mai said, so softly he could barely hear her above the horse's hoofs. "We had our moment."

"And it was wonderful."

"Hold on," she said. "Haaw!" The horses broke into a gallop. The trail had widened and turned away from the edge, sloping slightly downhill. Suddenly the horses were in the air! The landing came hard and Rain threw Rip.

A juniper that somehow had managed to take root on a ledge took most of the impact. Rip yelled.

Mai untangled him a few seconds later. "Anything broken?"

"Doesn't seem like it," Rip said, as she helped him to his feet. "Was that the worst?"

"Yes."

"What did we jump over?"

"A drop . . . four hundred feet down."

"Thank goodness it's too dark to see," Rip said.

"Do you need help getting back on Rain?" Mai asked.

Rip didn't answer; instead he pulled Mai to him and kissed her. "I'm sorry I left you. I wish we could go back there . . . "

"As Tahoma would say, 'Too many sunsets have passed, and the light is all different now.' But hold me for a minute. I miss your dangerous arms around me."

"That warm breeze . . . " Rip said, kissing her again.

She let their mouths linger, then pulled back. "Maybe it wasn't our moment, maybe it was just the winds of change." Mai climbed onto her horse. "We'd better go. There's still some steep ground to cover."

Rip got back on Rain. "It's cold," he said.

"Don't worry, I brought blankets." Mai said, and although he couldn't see it, he heard the smile in her voice.

fifty

Wrapped in one of Mai's woven blankets, Rip paced to keep warm against the cold desert night. Finally, a faint whisper of light transformed the sky to indigo. "It'll be light in an hour," Mai said.

"Where are they?" Rip asked again. Waiting for Gale was suicide. At any minute choppers could break across the sky and flood the area with lights. Tension Rock had been a good choice, with its cascading boulders and numerous small caves. Even the horses were concealed, and yet the hideout afforded a decent view of the trail and beyond, over the rim.

"It's a big canyon," she repeated.

"How can he search in the dark?"

"Day or night the canyon is the same. Tahoma knows the sounds as well as the sights. A breeze sings a different song in each tree. Stillness whispers a unique hush at every spot. Nothing is ever the same. We don't merely see with our eyes."

He'd seen her use just those skills to navigate their way along the steep trail and finally to where they now hid. "I can't wait much longer. She'd want me to protect the Eysen."

Headlights suddenly split the blackness. Rip couldn't tell where they were coming from.

"It's Tahoma," Mai said. "His truck sounds like no other."

Rip could barely hear it and, even if he could, he would not have been able to tell the difference between it and any other pickup. But he trusted Mai and followed her to meet the vehicle.

Gale jumped out and ran into his arms. "I thought you'd be gone," she cried, while clutching the back of his neck.

"Not without my partner in crime." He said, surprised at his joy in holding her.

Gale kissed his neck and cheeks. "I'm glad you waited, even though you shouldn't have." She laughed, embarrassed by her display of emotion.

Her kisses sent his thoughts to Mai and made him self-conscious. "Now we have to go."

Rip turned and found Tahoma handing him keys. "Take my truck."

"I couldn't," Rip said.

"What? Are you going to make your escape on horseback? The horse is worth more than my truck. I only hope it gets you off the rez; it's never been that far."

Rip dug into his pack, trying to find Grinley's envelope of cash. "Here." He held out a thin stack of hundreds.

"Your money's no good here."

"Please take it."

"You'll need it more than I will."

"I've got more. Please, I won't take the truck without paying you something."

"Take it, Tahoma, please, so we can go," Gale said.

He took it and hugged Rip. "There's a map in the glove box," he said, then explained how to get to the main road.

Rip hugged Mai. "You're right, timing doesn't seem to be our thing," he said.

"Or maybe it is. Things have a way of knowing how they're supposed to work out. We don't always know what's best."

"I love you, Mai," he whispered in her ear.

"Then do something for me," she said. "Stay alive. I'd like to see you again, when there is time to see the sunrise."

"There will always be sunrises and I'm sure we'll find one . . . in this or another lifetime," Rip said, glad it made her smile.

"Go," Tahoma said.

For thirty-five minutes, they bounced along the rutted dirt roads trying to follow Tahoma's directions. Rip wished the old truck knew the way as the horses had. Finally, they found pavement, and headed southwest toward Flagstaff. Avoiding the interstate meant adding more than an hour to their trip, but it was their best shot.

In between navigating, Gale had avoided asking about Sean; intentionally keeping the conversation on their adventures in the night, but as the road stretched ahead of them and the sun rose, she summoned her courage.

"He's dead."

"I was afraid of that," she said in a shaky voice.

"He fell trying to climb a rock wall high enough to get a signal on his phone."

"Poor Sean."

"He was trying to get us captured."

"Because they tricked him and he didn't know us well enough to trust that we hadn't killed Josh."

"I know."

"His parents will be devastated. Two innocent sons, dead."

"The cost of the Eysen is astonishing."

"Let's not discuss that again."

"I sometimes wonder if I did the right thing. Maybe if I'd listened to Larsen and handled the find like any other, the Eysen would be being studied right now by a team of top scientists from around the world."

"Do you really believe that?"

"No. But Larsen, Josh, Topper, Grinley, and Sean would still be alive."

"I doubt that. The only difference is that you'd be dead too."

fifty-one

Agents reported to Busman what he already knew. Gaines was gone. Sean's death also wasn't a surprise. When the phone stopped emitting its signal, they knew something went wrong and operatives were sent to investigate. The signs had been there: Sean was too emotional, immature, and not bright enough to pull off his mission. They considered him a lottery ticket; great if it paid off, if not, no big deal, just tear it up and buy another. Busman wasn't worried; he had lots of tickets.

He checked the monitor on his laptop and saw a satellite image of the pickup truck traveling toward Tuba City on 264. Although he currently couldn't see the occupants, he had no doubt that Gale and Rip were in the vehicle. One of Sean's first assignments had been to place tracking devices in their packs, and that part he'd done well. And even though there was a slim chance that Gale would win her argument for Colorado, Busman had already bet heavily on Flagstaff. Busman did one hundred push-ups; then contacted his lead field operative. Everything needed to go perfectly.

The NSA had been well represented in Flagstaff for several days. Operatives were ready to thwart the Vatican and FBI attempts at apprehending Gaines. Those two groups were sophisticated and certainly required attention, but neither the FBI Director, nor the Cardinal running the Church's operation had any idea what they faced. The NSA had become unimaginably powerful by dominating the collection and dissection of the most important commodity in history – information.

Perhaps only Booker knew how dangerous the NSA could be. He'd been obsessed with knowledge and information since childhood. And he'd played with the NSA plenty over the years. They traded information and had grown powerful together. But their aims had ended up being quite different.

At one time, the NSA took action in order to provide the intelligence community with the tools needed to make decisions; namely, intelligence. As the years passed, the NSA had access to so much information that managing it required judgments as the data was collected, rather than when disseminated. Soon, they began deciding every manner of national security question, such as which American citizens could be trusted and which were likely to cause problems. And the definition of "problems" became broader and broader. Their reach was everywhere, even into the White House.

Booker called it his deal with the devil. "It was like swimming with a shark," he told those closest to him. "I've got to keep going toward shore, while trying not to get eaten alive." He, like so many others, had once been an asset, and now was a threat. The Vatican felt the same way about him, and the NSA was unable to decide which party was the devil in that deal. But now there was a clash among titans. And in order to win, each needed to use the very thing they were fighting over. "It's a Catch-22 from hell," Booker said.

"It shouldn't be this hard," Booker told Kruse. "Gaines is gone again. The NSA let him slip away. He should have come straight to me after the find, but somehow Gale Asher convinced him not to trust me."

"Flagstaff?"

"Yeah, we've already got people on the ground, but I want you guys there also. The extraction team is going to try to catch up with him along the way. And I've got a nice little surprise in store for Rip, but it may backfire. Either way, Flagstaff is likely our last shot. Get there!"

A DIRT agent expressed the Director's regrets to Barbeau and Hall in Flagstaff. "There won't be any way to see Grinley. He's concerned about the NSA getting their hands on him."

"I need to know what Grinley knows!" Barbeau was incensed.

"Do you trust the Director?" the DIRT agent asked.

"The Director himself told me to trust no one!"

fifty-two

"My dad has a place in Mexico that no one knows about," Rip said, as they rolled along the quiet highway. "He doesn't own it, but it's his. Some weird arrangement with the locals."

"A tax dodge?"

"No. My father does not do anything unless it's legal."

"But he'll help us?"

"He's my dad." Rip smiled, thinking about how few subjects he and his father agreed on. In spite of that, he was the one person on whom Rip could always rely. "We need gas soon. I think our next chance is Tuba City. I'll call him from there."

There were three payphones mounted to a wall on the side of the old service station; two were missing the handsets, and luckily, the third worked.

"I thought I might hear from you," his father said. "Are you okay?"

"Yeah, but I need a favor."

"And you want to ask it over the phone?"

"I don't really have a choice."

"Okay. How about we talk about that time we went fishing?"

"Which time?" Rip asked.

His father remained silent.

"Oh, that time," Rip felt foolish for not knowing what his father meant.

"And the guy at that place?" his father asked.

"Yeah."

"Okay. And that time in Los Angeles with the couple from New York."

"New Jersey?"

"You're right, New Jersey. But, you know when I mean?"

"Yeah, as long as we're talking about Jersey."

"We are. Now, let's see. Okay. Take the amount of your first allowance. Add to that the number of kittens in Chloe's first litter. And then the number of Lola's cars."

"Got it."

"That would take care of what you want, right?"

"Yes, Dad, thanks. And you don't mind doing this?"

"Well, I'd rather be doing just about anything else, but you know . . . "

"Rise to the occasion," Rip finished his father's words.

"Yeah, we gotta do what needs doing."

"At the place, where we were that time?"

"I'll be there."

"And Dad, make sure neither of you are followed."

"Likewise."

Rip hung up and was about to head back to the truck, when he heard a familiar voice call his name.

He turned and let out a gasp as if he'd been punched, unable to believe the man standing in front of him was really there. "Are you, you?" Rip stuttered.

"The reports of my death have been greatly exaggerated," Larsen Fretwell said.

"How?" Rip's voice was strained.

"It wasn't me on the catwalk in Atlanta."

"How is that possible? It was all over the news."

"Can't always believe what you see on TV," Larsen smiled, but then his expression turned serious. "Booker did lose two men in the accident. Two men who died, trying to save me."

"What happened?"

"Booker's guys pulled me out of my beach house, before the FBI could arrest me or the Vatican agents, who were waiting there, could kill me. It was hot pursuit after that and Booker sent in a decoy crew. He had a big tall fellow like me fly to Atlanta with another guy. I think initially the feds thought it had been me, but they surely would have figured it out by the next day. I'm not sure why they withheld the truth from the media."

Rip shook his head. "But how did you get away?"

"Harmer, one of Booker's hired guns, and I got offshore in a speedboat. We eventually wound up in Cuba."

"Cuba?"

"Booker has a place there."

"And, all this time?"

"I've been waiting for you. But Booker says you've decided not to trust him anymore and thought I might be able to convince you that he's on our side."

"Well, that's a great idea, except I'm not sure I trust you either."

"Are you joking?"

"You're my best friend, I'm thrilled you're alive; shocked, but truly ecstatic. It's just that another person I trusted just tried to get me killed, and then there's the little matter of you bringing Gale to the dig site in the first place, and lying to me about your relationship with her."

"She told you, huh?"

Rip nodded.

"Man, I'm sorry about that. If I'd known what was going to happen, I would have told you. At the time, I just didn't want you to be mad at me. It didn't seem important to get into a scene in front of everyone."

"You could have told me before I left with her," he said, still stunned to be speaking to his "dead" best friend.

"She and I had a big fight about that. I didn't want her to go. Everything happened so fast. We had no idea it was going to turn into this crazy nightmare."

"You wouldn't believe it if I told you," Rip said. "Either way, Larsen, I'm glad you're alive."

"Me too." Larsen tossed a phone to Rip. "Just talk to Booker, please. He's on speed-dial one, and the phone is scrambled."

Rip caught it and stared at the phone a second. "Okay. But first tell me, how did you find us?"

"I found Tahoma. *He* still trusts me and gave me the plate number to his truck." He pointed over his shoulder with his thumb. "Mind if I go say hello to Gale? I can't wait to see the look on her face."

Rip did kind of mind. And he still had a million questions for Larsen, but time was short. He remembered Clastier's words about trust. He wanted to trust Larsen, and he needed to trust Booker. They already knew his location, so there wasn't much to lose. "Sure, go ahead," he said, pushing the button on the phone.

fifty-three

Larsen disappeared around the corner to find Gale, as Booker answered the phone.

"You wanted to talk to me," Rip said.

"Rip, god damn it," Booker said. "Who in the hell convinced you I was your enemy?"

"Well . . . "

"Well, don't you know I'm the best friend you have in the world?"

"West Memphis?"

"What about it?"

"You were the only one who knew where we were."

"You've got to be kidding. They traced the rental, Rip. They did some sort of grid sort on every car rented within a certain radius and tracked them all. The Vatican guys got lucky and made it there first. The fact that you're still alive *and* free might say different, but the FBI does actually know what they're doing, and they're sharing info with the Vatican. But you've got much bigger problems than them."

"You don't have to tell me."

"Oh, I think I do. The NSA is watching you right now. They've got transmitters in your packs, but don't go getting rid of them until you're ready for them to flock in for the kill, because they'll know the minute you do."

"If the NSA wants the artifacts so badly, and they know where I am, how come I'm still free?"

"And alive," Booker emphasized. "They need your knowledge; they want to make sure they know everything you do, before they kill you."

Rip's mind went blank for a moment. He felt as if he had to remember to breathe, or his lungs might collapse under the sheer weight of the armies amassed against him.

"Rip, I can get you out."

"Where will we go? You said they're watching." Rip wasn't sure what to believe, but he desperately wanted to trust Booker.

"They are. We have a plan. I assume you're heading to Flagstaff. Don't worry. This phone is scrambled and untraceable. They can pick up your end from the payphone, but it'll be twenty-four hours until that gets done."

"How do you know all this?"

"I sell them the damned equipment."

"Of course you do."

"Anyway, you can't go with Larsen. The NSA would close in on us all in ten seconds. But Larsen will give you a GPS unit; the coordinates are programmed in, and a time is written on the back. An extraction team will be there to get you. Ten minutes before the meet, find a vehicle to put your tracking devices in. That's the tricky part, so do it smoothly."

"Okay, I can do that."

"You actually have plenty of time. The Vatican and the FBI have no idea where you are. The NSA is keeping them at bay."

"I should go; I feel better moving. I've gotten kind of used to it."

"We'll put an end to that, my friend. It's almost over. But before you hang up, I need to tell you about your biggest problem."

When Rip arrived back at the truck, now with a full tank, and pulled under one of the few trees in sight, he found Larsen and Gale in serious conversation. She'd been crying.

"Am I interrupting something?" he asked, coolly.

Gale looked at him with pleading eyes. He knew better than to let himself get trapped in the blue. "We need to go."

Larsen looked from Gale to Rip. "Look, guys, no need for all this tension. We're all still alive."

"Yeah, but you're the only one who's known that for the past two weeks," Rip said. "I've been living with the guilt of your death. And while we're talking about being alive, there are others who haven't been so lucky."

"Rip, don't make me out to be the bad guy just because I didn't die. I begged you not to take the damned Eysen."

"I told you so? You came back from the dead to say I told you so?"

"No, I'm just saying lay off; we're in this now. Let's get it done the right way. Booker is the only hope."

"We've been doing just fine up until now without his help," Gale said.

"Fine? You call people getting killed fine?" Larsen asked.

"Tell me why, after all the years we worked on Cosega, when we finally found it, you were afraid?" Rip asked.

"I wasn't the one afraid, Rip. You were. I had faith that if we followed the procedures we'd been trained in, the same ones we'd always done, then everything would be fine. What is the good of finding Cosega, if you're going to hide it from the world?"

"After all this, you don't realize. This. Is. Not. A. Normal. Find!"

"You're the one who made it not normal," Larsen yelled back. "You attracted all of this trouble."

Rip took a deep breath. "Maybe. But there's a whole lot you don't know."

"I'm sure there is. Maybe you'll explain it all to me while we're sitting on one of Booker's islands trying to make sense of it," Larsen said, smiling. "I don't want to argue with you, Rip. I came here to rescue you. Whatever mistakes we've made don't matter now."

"Shouldn't we be going?" Gale asked, looking back up the highway.

"Here, take this." Larsen handed him the GPS. Rip turned it over and read the time.

"I need time to think," Rip said.

"You've got hours," Larsen replied.

"How did you get here?" Rip asked.

"Helicopter."

"How come we didn't hear it," Gale asked.

"I got here first."

"How'd you know we were going to stop?"

"Have you seen any other gas stations?" Larsen smiled.

"Where's the copter now?"

"They'll be back as soon as I call them."

fifty-four

Gale was relieved when they pulled away from the station without Larsen. For a minute she thought Rip was going to want them to go in the helicopter.

"What's with that?" she asked, pointing to the GPS.

"To help us navigate."

"How'd the call with your father go?"

"I couldn't reach him."

"Then where are we going?" Gale asked surprised.

"I've got a friend in Sedona. He can help."

"How? Why don't we just head north, when we get to 89? We could be in Colorado tonight. Lost in the mountains. Figure out the Eysen, the Odeon, you could tell me more about what was in Clastier's letters . . . "

"No. We have to get out of the country."

"I don't understand why you're so angry. Your best friend, who you thought was dead, is alive. And instead of hugging him, you practically took his head off."

"I'm not in the mood to talk right now. I need to think."

"You know what? When you're not in the mood to talk, that's when you need to talk the most. And you know what else I think? I think you're a little jealous of Larsen."

"Jealous? Why would I be jealous?"

"Because he and I were dating."

"Oh, don't flatter yourself, Gale. Go ahead and resume your relationship with Larsen; it's fine with me."

"Really? Well, it's nice to know how you feel."

"I didn't know there was any question."

Gale drove faster, glad she was too angry to cry. "What did Booker have to say?"

"Booker?"

"Yeah. Larsen told me you were talking to him. Any reason you didn't want to tell me about it?"

"No reason, I just hadn't gotten around to it. We've been busy talking about how much you missed dating Larsen."

"What's your problem?"

"I've got half the world chasing me, the other half lying to me, and most of them want me dead."

"Don't you mean chasing *us*?"

"Look, Gale, I don't see you getting charged with murder."

"The charges were dropped."

"Whatever, I took the artifacts. They want me. For all I know, they think you're my hostage."

"I thought we were in this together. Clastier is important to me. I've seen inside the Eysen. I'm here!"

"But you knew none of this three weeks ago. I was just a name on your list of interview topics. The Eysen, Clastier, they didn't exist for you."

"You're just talking about days of the week. Time isn't that simple. As soon as I learned what I know, I've always known it."

"What the hell does that mean?" Rip asked, focusing on the heat blurring off the asphalt that seemed like a black ribbon through an otherwise desolate moonscape of diagonal cliffs, jagged rocks, and miles of meaningless barbed wire.

"Haven't you read what Clastier said about time?" Gale asked, adjusting the visor to avoid the glare of the sun.

"Of course I have, I've read it a hundred times."

"Then why don't you know what I'm talking about?" Gale asked.

"Because everyone reads Clastier differently."

"What?"

"The earlier Clastier church builders discovered it. They had study groups so that they could better interpret and understand his words. Soon, after some arguing, they realized they weren't reading the same things. I mean the words were the same, but they each got totally different meanings from them," Rip said.

"You don't think reincarnation is real, yet you believe that the nineteenth century writings of a defrocked priest can change, dependent on the reader, and you've witnessed an eleven-million-year-old computer show images of *us* from this lifetime!"

"It's easier to believe the changing, multi-meanings of Clastier's writings, his prophecies, and even the Eysen, because there is proof I can see." Rip slammed his hand on the dashboard. "Reincarnation is impossible . . . at least it was until my encounters with the shopkeeper and Sani-Niyol. Now, you'll be happy to know, although I don't pretend to understand it, I do believe there is something to it."

"It's about time."

"I damn sure hope there's more to this than my atoning for Conway's sins. Some strange karmic twist that

I'm now trying to save Clastier's work, that I, in another life, once fought so hard to destroy."

"I think you know there is far more to it than that," Gale said tensely.

fifty-five

Pisano wore a Fioravanti suit; it was the most important meeting of his life. He recognized all but two women, as he looked nervously around the room, unsure why the President of the United States had called this emergency summit. Obviously, he knew the topic, but he didn't see the point of bringing these people of widely diverse interests together to discuss the Eysen. The Vatican's position was "non-negotiable," as the Pope believed that both the Malachy Prophecies and Clastier's Divinations gave the Vatican undeniable ownership to the Eysen.

The President entered and quickly turned the meeting over to Kristi Toft, whose title, Special Counsel to the President, could mean just about anything. Pisano noticed the delicate gold chain that disappeared under her blue cotton blouse and wondered if there was a cross on the end. By the end of the day, he would have a complete file on her, but now he could only speculate. She was attractive, in a delicate way, but firm and capable in her manner; not surprising given the position to which she'd risen. He could tell she was smarter than he was and he'd disliked her immediately, but consoled himself knowing he was the best dressed in the room.

Toft efficiently introduced the participants who included the Directors of the FBI and the CIA, Attorney General Dover, a woman from the NSA, Booker Lipton, and Pisano. Booker had reluctantly agreed to attend at the insistence of the President. Noticeably absent was Senator Monroe. Booker and Pisano were the only non-governmental attendees. Pisano didn't feel outnumbered; his constituency represented nearly twenty percent of the world's population. After the introductions, Toft told them she wanted each to explain their interest in the Eysen and asked Pisano to go first.

"The Holy Father has laid claim to the object you call 'the Eysen' for centuries. It belongs to the Vatican."

"How do you figure?" the CIA Director asked. "It was found on American soil."

"Our claim predates the existence of America by more than five hundred years. The fact that it was found here means no more than the location of a stolen masterpiece painting. It belongs to the owner from which it was taken."

"Are you saying we stole the Eysen from the Vatican?" the CIA Director asked, sounding annoyed.

"If the Eysen is not returned to the Vatican, then yes, that's exactly what I'm saying."

"Please," Toft said, "we're not here to argue. The President called this summit so that we could work together toward the two objectives we all agree on: first, to avoid additional players entering the field, and second, to keep the media contained."

"If it weren't for the FBI's sloppy handling of the investigation, this would have been wrapped up long ago," Pisano said.

"Mr. Pisano, the Vatican agents have obstructed the Bureau since day one. I might also question the NSA's involvement –"

"Enough," Dover said.

"Yes," the CIA Director agreed. "The issue is not what has happened up until now. If you think things have been crowded before this, it is about to get much worse. We have picked up chatter that the Chinese, Russians, and Israelis are aware of the operation."

"Your leaks are an embarrassment," Pisano said.

"Do they know the nature of the object?" Booker asked.

"Leaks, wherever they're coming from, may be an embarrassment, Mr. Pisano," the woman from the NSA said; "however, the results are a problem for us *all*."

"We don't know how much they know, Booker," the CIA Director said; he'd met Booker many times. "But it's likely the Chinese and the Israelis are closer to understanding than the Russians. There is some evidence that the Israelis have actually been aware of the Eysen, prior to Gaines locating it."

Booker nodded. He had to get Gaines out of the country now. Navigating the U.S. intelligence agencies was difficult enough, but he had many contacts. He had billions invested in China and was well connected there, but the Communist government's competing interests would limit his ability to gain an edge. The other problem presented by Chinese involvement was that it was one of the few countries that could outspend Booker. Although he wasn't without resources in Israel, their participation would make things much tougher, especially if they really did know precisely what it was that everyone wanted.

"I don't know why we're here wasting time," Pisano said. "You all can resolve your internal power struggles and stop stepping on each other's feet. But you don't need us and it's irrelevant. Even if an agency of the U.S. Government, or one of its citizens," he nodded to Booker, "obtains the Eysen before our agents, the Vatican will use all means available to regain possession."

"Good luck with that," the Director of the CIA said.

"Gentlemen, ladies," said the President, who had remained silent until then. "We're aware of the tools at the Vatican's disposal. It need not get to that. We must come to an agreement of what will become of the Eysen, whenever it is recovered. And then, we will share information to make sure that one of us gets the damned thing, before the Chinese, Israelis, Russians, or someone even worse. We are not leaving this room until there is an agreement."

Everyone looked at Pisano, except Booker, who stared directly at the woman from the NSA.

"Mr. President," Pisano said, reveling in the attention, "do you honestly think we can work together? You people don't even trust each other. How on earth do you expect us to trust you?"

"I'm not sure you understand, Mr. Pisano. I wasn't making a request," the President said.

"With all due respect, I answer to a higher authority," Pisano said, smirking. "And perhaps you're unaware, but your own NSA has sent look-alikes out there to distract the FBI, and the FBI has detained NSA and Vatican agents. The FBI is withholding information from your Attorney General, and Booker Lipton has people running around in all directions. No one trusts anyone."

"Of course, I am aware of this. That is precisely why I summoned all the parties. Do you think the Vatican can, by itself, do what it has failed to do for the past ten days?"

"As I said, if your people would get out of our way, we'd have Gaines in a few hours."

The CIA Director scoffed.

The FBI Director had not uttered a word. He knew too much. The President was mostly using the summit to put Booker and the Vatican on notice that they were going to lose this. The President, at the bequest of the NSA, had wanted everything on the table and used the Russians, Chinese, and Israelis to scare various participants into complying. As far as the FBI Director knew, only the Israelis were close enough to pose a real threat. They, like the Vatican, had known about the Eysen prior to the discovery.

In spite of the President's strong-arming, the meeting adjourned with only an agreement to meet again in three days, if the Eysen had not been recovered, but no one expected that to be the case. Each party had reason to believe that they would be in possession of the powerful artifact by the end of the day.

fifty-six

Rip hadn't been sure how or when he would bring up what he'd learned from Booker. Normally that kind of information would take him days to process. "A scientist is trained to evaluate data and reach conclusions based on facts; emotion merely gets in the way," he'd once told a past girlfriend. That relationship, like the few others he'd attempted, hadn't lasted. But Gale was different. She was not a girlfriend; although he couldn't deny he had developed feelings of some sort and found the way she caused him to see things within himself, and the world, exciting.

Larsen had foolishly told her he was talking to Booker, which probably meant Larsen didn't know what Booker had told him. In either case, it forced him to address the ugly truth and the timing could not have been worse.

"Booker told me that the Church had people on my digs, watching, informing," Rip said, checking his pack for the fifth time, while Gale drove.

"What are you saying?"

"Someone at that camp was a Vatican plant!"

"My God, who?"

"Exactly. You tell me."

"How would I know?"

"Maybe you should ask Senator Monroe, better known as the next President. I'm sure he could tell us."

"What does he have to do with this?"

"Really? That's how you're going to play this, Gale? After all we've been through, I hoped for a shred of honesty!" He glared at her. She glanced back, her eyes suddenly helpless, breaths coming short.

"I don't know what you're talking about."

"How do you lie so easily? I know about you and Senator Monroe!"

"What about us?"

"You were lovers!"

"That was fifteen years ago. I don't have to give you a history of my love life!"

"Not a whole history. There aren't enough hours for that. But in case you've forgotten, the Vatican is trying to kill me, and your boyfriend, Senator Monroe, is best buddies with the Pope. That was probably worth mentioning!"

"I didn't tell you about Monroe because it's ancient history and had no relevance to our situation."

"No relevance! When did you last talk to him?"

"I'm not sure."

"Come on, Gale, think about it. You and I met on July 10th, so go from there."

"I guess it was on the ninth," she said softly.

"What? Could you speak a little louder? I'm not sure the NSA's mics can hear you when you whisper."

She just looked at him.

"Don't, Gale. You have the audacity to look at me as if *you've* been betrayed. You talked to Monroe the day before I found the Eysen, and you pretend that it didn't matter.

Do you know he regularly meets with Vatican officials? And what about his nickname, Senator NSA?"

"His opponents call him that for political gain."

"Because it's true; he is the agency's greatest champion. Your lover is big brother; he's the God-damned Antichrist. How could you?"

"I didn't do anything wrong. I even thought of calling him to help us."

"That's so funny, it's not even funny. Gale, I don't believe anything you say. You kept your relationship with Larsen secret. Now the Senator, and Sean Stadler, were they ever on our side, or were they working with the NSA from the start?"

"The NSA?"

"Don't tell me you didn't know." Rip couldn't stop his anger. "I do have one question for you. And, if you're capable of honesty, I'd really appreciate knowing. That first day, were you the one who called from the camp and told what we found?"

"I can't believe you'd even ask me that." Gale clenched her fists around the wheel, determined not to cry.

"You had access to Larsen's satphone. Did you call Monroe? The FBI? Were you the Vatican plant?"

"Go to hell, Rip!"

"Oh, you'd like that, wouldn't you? Has that been the plan all along? Find out everything I know, and then kill me?"

"You're so confused."

"Damn right I'm confused. Being surrounded by nothing but lies tends to do that to a person. Sean traps us, wants to kill me, you with Larsen, with Monroe . . . Senator freaking NSA! Man, it's hard to believe, I actually . . . All you've done for days is try to poison me against the one person who could help me, not coincidently also the person who could tell me the truth about you."

"You're wrong."

"I wish I were, Gale," he said, trying to calm down. "But even if you were innocent, and all of this soap opera was an awful coincidence, how do I know what else you haven't told me? I mean, come on, you're sleeping with the enemy. Tell me what you would think, if you were me?"

"I would believe the good and not the bad. I would do what Clastier says . . . trust."

fifty-seven

For more than an hour, there had been only the sound of the rattling engine of Tahoma's old truck, and the tires rolling along the sun-baked asphalt. Gale and Rip both tried to make sense of Larsen being alive, Sean being dead, the Monroe drama, and the complex ramifications of it all. They rode in rigid silence until, just outside Flagstaff, Gale pulled into an empty parking lot in front of an abandoned building that looked like it might have once been a carpet store. She stepped onto the broken blacktop that had mostly been reclaimed by weeds.

"What's this?" Rip asked, ready to pull out Grinley's gun. His eyes darted. "Is this where someone kills me?"

Gale shook her head, squinted her eyes in disbelief, tossed him the car keys, turned, and walked away.

Rip jumped out. "Where are you going?"

"Away from you," she said, adjusting her pack.

Rip didn't know what to say, wasn't sure what to do. He watched her going down the highway for a minute, before calling after her, "It's not safe to be out there walking around in broad daylight. They know we're going to Flagstaff. Come back, let's talk about this." He couldn't believe that he was calling her back.

"I'll be fine." She waved over her shoulder.

He thought for a minute. Gale would be fine. Monroe would protect her. Maybe that's why she'd been so cool throughout all of this; she was never in any danger. He watched her get farther away, still unsure. Gale's leaving confirmed her guilt; she was too smart to just go on a suicide run. Rip got back in the car. He had to meet the extraction team. Gale didn't know about that. No one did. It was almost over now.

Rip, determined to speed by, slowed down when he caught up to her. He yelled across the open lane between them. "Are you sure?" Again, surprised to be involuntarily giving her another chance.

"Good luck, Rip."

"You, too," was all he could think to say, before stepping on the accelerator. He followed her in the rearview mirror until she was lost to the heat-blurred horizon.

"Damn," he said out loud. "If I can't figure out that whole mess with Gale, how am I going to understand the Cosega sequence? How will I make sense out of the Eysen at all?"

Gale walked on the gravely shoulder, numb with shock, unaccustomed to being exposed, feeling like a girl skipping school, except that nefarious people lurked in every shadow. Second-guessing every decision since that day so long ago when she'd accepted the invitation of her then-professor Monroe. Hers had been a serious crush, but she had never expected to cross the line. And dating Larsen, that had definitely been a mistake, even though it led her to the Eysen and the Clastier Papers. She should have told Rip about Larsen, and especially about Monroe, early on;

she could have explained them a hundred different ways. Things are better up front, without anger and fear.

Sean was a different matter altogether. The Stadler brothers had been the most innocent victims in the whole crisis. Even Topper knew, after a lifetime of guarding secrets, that danger was never far from his door. But the Stadler brothers had wandered into the storm thinking the world was a gentle place filled with laughter and pretty places. Gale felt the worst about them.

She'd seen a billboard for a motel a few miles back, so she knew there wasn't far to walk. Low on cash, since Rip had Grinley's envelope, she would be able to stay only one night, but that gave her about twenty hours to take a long bath, to sleep, and to find a solution.

fifty-eight

Rip followed the GPS instructions and arrived near the meeting point almost a full hour before the extraction team was going to pull him out by helicopter. Fifteen minutes earlier, while at a truck stop, he'd found the tracking device in his pack. It had not been easy to find, and if he hadn't known about it; the flexible quarter-sized chip would have remained undetected.

He came across a driver checking his load and struck up a conversation; the guy was heading to San Diego. Rip managed to get the tracking device into the cab; then watched as the semi drove away.

It was then that he realized Gale's tracking device was still in her pack. Even if she wasn't working with them, the NSA now knew the two of them had separated. And, if she were actually a Vatican agent, then everyone knew, except maybe the FBI. He still didn't understand all the connections and the shady double-deals, as mighty powers jockeyed to get their hands on the Eysen. While thinking about Gale's role, it occurred to him that maybe he hadn't been the only one looking for the Eysen all these years. Many had been waiting for it. How did they know? If there were two Eysens, there could be three, ten, even a hundred. But then, why did the NSA need him? Maybe they were like nukes, every country needed one to maintain a balance of power. Gale could be working for anyone, or the prospect which bothered him most, she could be innocent.

Fortunately, Booker's people had chosen a low, flat field for the helicopter to land. The location allowed Rip to find a spot in the hills about a quarter of a mile away. He hiked to a concealed vantage point and watched. Gale had been right about one thing: Rip was confused. He didn't know what to believe about her, Sean, or Larsen; but the biggest mystery remained – Booker. Had Gale been working to instigate his distrust of Booker, or had it been the other way around? Did Booker tell him all those things so he would no longer trust Gale? He didn't know anything for sure, except that he couldn't afford to follow Clastier's advice on trust. Too many people were after him. The extraction, his best chance of escape, could be the latest trick; another trap to get him. This time, he would play it smart and do his own stakeout.

It didn't take long before the FBI arrived and took up hidden positions around the field. Rip almost cried. Gale had been right. Booker's betrayal was no longer a possibility, but rather a reality. In the hours since Larsen had given him the GPS with the time taped on the back, no one could have known about the extraction location. They had taken the precautions to set up the meeting by using the GPS to avoid any specifics on the phone. Only Booker knew all the details, and now, the FBI was waiting to arrest him. He watched a dozen agents, most with FBI emblazoned on their backs, disappear into the underbrush and trees bordering the field, and he wondered what Booker had received in exchange for him.

Rip crouched behind a tree, devastated. He also realized there was a new problem; he had to be careful getting out of there. They wouldn't be expecting him to show up for another forty minutes, but there were a ton of agents in the area. Carefully making his way back to Tahoma's truck, he worried that it would already be swarming with FBI agents. This time he got lucky; the pick-up sat alone, just where he had left it, and it even started on the first try.

He still had about four hours to kill before the meeting with his father, his last real shot at escaping. Gale knew his dad had a place in Mexico, but it would be very hard to trace. Even so, it presented a problem, one he didn't know how to address. Gale was a real puzzle. Nothing Booker said could be believed, and yet she did admit to a relationship with Senator Monroe, a man known to be a close ally of the Vatican, the NSA, and even the FBI. She had concealed her relationship, not only with the Senator, but the whole Larsen affair, and her defense of Sean. Part of him wanted to forget he ever knew her, and the other part wanted to go find Gale and bring her to Mexico. But in the end, protecting the Eysen was more important than anything.

Rip drove to a primitive Forest Service road, not far from the airfield, where he would be meeting his father and Dyce, an old family friend with a small plane, who regularly flew to Mexico. Assuming a ranger didn't happen by, not likely with an underfunded USFS, he could wait out the time undisturbed. The truck was concealed from the air by a thick canopy of evergreens and Rip felt quite safe. He considered using the time to study the Eysen; then decided he didn't feel *that* safe. After a few minutes, he made a decision that would totally undermine Busman's carefully constructed plans.

fifty-nine

The newswoman spoke in the official monotone voice that local anchors often use for serious stories. "Famed archaeologist, Ripley Gaines, was killed today in a shootout with federal law enforcement. The bizarre case began ten days ago in Virginia with the professor's disappearance; he allegedly stole important artifacts that had been unearthed in the Jefferson National Forest. Gaines was subsequently charged with the murder of a lab worker, but those charges were later dropped. Viewers, please use discretion; the following footage contains graphic images of violence which some may find disturbing."

Gale sank to the floor of the motel room, but continued watching. Grainy images, seemingly filmed from a chopper, showed Rip running, stopping, pulling out a gun, and being shot several times. The screen switched to clearer images of a body covered in a sheet being loaded into an ambulance. She should have been there. "They killed him!" she cried.

Their final minutes together had been consumed by stupid fighting. She wanted to go back and do it all differently. "Rip. I'm sorry, Rip!" she wailed. A long time passed before she stopped crying and found the strength to get off the floor. "The Eysen is lost," she thought. "It might be time to surrender."

But then she remembered the Clastier Papers. She still had them, along with the notes in her journal about the letters. They could not fall into the wrong hands. And now, she and Teresa were the only ones who knew of the missing papers and a second Eysen. Rip had told her about an old lost church where Clastier had begun. He said Clastier's friend, Padre Garcia of the Church at Las Trampas, not far from Taos, had received other letters. Could she go back? Would they still be after her, now that the Eysen had been recovered?

No one knew where she was. But now certain things were needed; a scrambled cell phone, money, a car, a computer, and a weapon. She had to get back to Teresa. Only one person could help her. Gale looked at the hotel phone on the bed stand. "What would he think when he heard her voice?" she thought, dialing the number. Was it even safe to call him? She would never have made the call if Rip were still alive.

sixty

Rip, suddenly worried that Larsen or Gale might have put a tracking device somewhere on the truck, had driven in the opposite direction and walked more than eight miles to the abandoned airstrip. The two-hour walk allowed plenty of thinking time, but yielded no more answers. He still managed to use his new tactic and arrived early, but to his surprise, a plane already stood waiting. He watched intently for ten minutes and saw only a single pilot. As the meeting time came and went, he wondered why his father hadn't shown up. Without binoculars, he couldn't be sure if the pilot was his dad's friend, Hence. But he had to do something; he knew the FBI and NSA were close, and it wouldn't take them long to find him.

He slowly made his way across the rocky terrain. He came to a shallow pool he hadn't seen from above. A short cliff rose from one end, and a thicket of cactus and vines was on the other side. He'd have to wade through it.

The gunshots popped at the same time he saw the men. A black man in a blue FBI ball cap fell, fifteen feet in front of him. Rip instinctively ran, splashing in the opposite direction, but was stopped by the cliff. Just as he was looking for a way to climb, he heard a man yell.

"Don't move, Gaines," a husky voice said. "I'll kill you, too. I don't care."

Rip raised his arms and turned around. The stocky man smiled.

"You have something that belongs to the Vatican," Leary said. "I assume it's in your pack?"

"Why does the Catholic Church think it belongs to them?" he asked, trying to buy time, searching for an escape.

"You don't get to ask questions," Leary said. "Give me the pack."

Rip thought about Grinley's gun. Maybe he could get this guy to let him open the pack to get the Eysen, and instead; he'd pull out the gun and shoot him. Rip had never shot anyone, but in this case he'd be more than willing. "It's fragile, I'll get it out," he said.

"Don't play games with me, Gaines. It's over! Walk slowly to the edge of the pool, take the pack off, and place it carefully on the ground in front of you."

Rip, trying to think, didn't move.

"Do it!" Leary cocked his Ruger and took a step toward Rip.

Rip looked over at the bleeding FBI agent, and for the first time, wished he'd been arrested. At least being taken into custody by the feds, he might have had a chance at living; at getting the word out about the Eysen and Clastier. "Okay, I'm coming," Rip took deliberate steps, still hoping to come up with a solution, his eyes scanning wildly, looking for an escape. Nothing.

"Come on, Gaines."

Rip made his way gradually to the edge of the pool.

"That's far enough," Leary said. "Take it off slowly."

Still standing in water, Rip could not think of anything to do. He took off the pack and carefully placed it on the ground beside the pool.

"You realize the Church is going to destroy the greatest artifact ever known to man?" Gaines said, trying to reason with an unreasonable man.

"Do you know who I work for?" Leary said, with a twisted smile.

"The Pope?"

Leary laughed. "I don't work for a man. I'm an agent of God." He took a step closer and aimed his pistol at Gaines' heart.

Rip looked over at the dead FBI agent, then at the pack. He had to do something.

Leary began chanting in Latin, "*Aspérges me. Dómine, hyssópo, et mundábor: lavábis me, et super nivem dealbábor.*" Then he spat on Hall's body. "You might not believe me, but I'm sad that you're never going to have a chance to meet God."

"I'm not interested in meeting *your* God," Gaines said.

Leary smirked. "Yeah, they'll have fun with you, where you're going. I'll give you ten seconds to confess your sins. One. Two. Three. Four. Five . . . "

Rip wished he had Grinley's gun, a rock, or anything. He thought again about running, but there was nowhere to go, and he was down to three seconds anyway.

"Eight. Nine. Ten." The shot rang deafeningly loud, an explosion of blood and flesh covered his chest and face. His last thought, before he collapsed into the water, was of the incomplete Cosega Sequence.

END OF BOOK 2

**COSEGA SHIFT, book three of the Cosega Sequence
is available at amazon.com**

Thank you for reading Cosega Storm! PLEASE, if you enjoyed my book, it would be a huge help if you could post a review on amazon.com. The number of reviews a book has, directly impacts sales. Nothing is more important to us indie authors than reviews. And, please tell your friends and find more of my books at amazon.com.

About the author

 Brandt Legg is a former child prodigy who turned an interest in stamp collecting into a multi-million dollar empire. At eight, Legg's father died suddenly, plunging his family into poverty. Two years later, while suffering from crippling migraines, he started in business. National media dubbed him the "Teen Tycoon," but by the time he reached his twenties, the high-flying Legg became ensnarled in the financial whirlwind of the junk bond eighties, lost his entire fortune... and ended up serving time in federal prison for financial improprieties. Legg emerged, chastened and wiser, one year later and began anew in retail and real estate. From there his life adventures have led him through magazine publishing, a newspaper column, photography, FM radio, CD production and concert promotion. He is also the best selling author of the Inner Movement trilogy. For more information, or to contact me, please visit my www.BrandtLegg.com

Contact the author

I'd love to hear from you. For more information, or to contact me, please visit my website www.BrandtLegg.com

Hear more from the author

If you want to be the first to hear about my new releases, please join my mailing list at www.BrandtLegg.com

Also by Brandt Legg

Outview (Inner Movement, book 1)
Outin (Inner Movement, book 2)
Outmove (Inner Movement, book 3)
The Complete Inner Movement trilogy

Cosega Search
Cosega Shift

Acknowledgements

Once again, there are many who have helped me get the Cosega Sequence books out. Roanne Legg, often save a plot point and got me back on track for my writing and otherwise. Barbara Blair, many times argued on behalf of the characters. And, Harriet Greene and Marty Goldman, who constructively cut into the first draft of the first book. Bonnie Brown Koeln and Elizabeth Chumney, who both generously taught me more about grammar than I learned during my entire freshman high school English class. A special thanks to Mike Sager for more than what is obvious. And finally to Teakki, who patiently waited, learning to read and making up his own stories, until I finished writing each day.

Printed in Great Britain
by Amazon.co.uk, Ltd.,
Marston Gate.